Double
Trouble at L'Etoile

School
for
Stars

Double
Trouble   at L'Etoile

School
for
Stars

Holly & Kelly
Willoughby

Orion
Children's Books

First published in Great Britain in 2015
by Orion Children's Books
an imprint of Hachette Children's Group
and published by Hodder and Stoughton Limited
Orion House
5 Upper St Martin's Lane
London WC2H 9EA
An Hachette UK Company

1 3 5 7 9 10 8 6 4 2

A catalogue record for this book is
available from the British Library

ISBN 978 1 4440 1455 6

www.orionchildrensbooks.co.uk

For moments when you feel like you're losing control. Have faith, Story-seeker. It's only a blip and when you come out the other side you'll be stronger than ever.

Contents

1   Together Again

2   Plenty To Dine Out About

3   Good Riddance To Bad Rubbish

4   An Icy Welcome

5   Get Your Skates On

6   A Sister's Love

7   Ever Get the Feeling You're Being
     Watched?

8   The Ghost

9   The Show Must Go On

10 Maria Makes Amends

11 An Unwelcome Spotter

12 The Hunt Is On

13 Special Agent Debrief

14 An Extra Invitation

15 So This Is How It's Going

    To Work . . .

16 Operation Snow White!

17 A Glimpse Into The Mind Of

    A Ghost

18 Operation Girl Versus Ghost

19 Operation What Happened On

    The Island!

20 Home Time Again

Welcome back, Story-seeker, to the start of a new school year at L'Etoile, School for Stars.

What a summer it's been, but time now for our girls to see what fun and mischief awaits them in the first term of their second year.

Term begins with the very unexpected departure of a naughty L'Etoilette which kicks off the gossip. Then, as ever, Madame Ruby has a surprise , which the girls can't wait to get their teeth into. Not to mention the arrival of two new students who are sure to throw the cat among the pigeons!

So if you want to know more, Story-seeker, then what are you waiting for? Get your skates on and glide back into the world of L'Etoile. You won't be disappointed!

Love
Holly and Kelly Willoughby x

1

Together Again

'I must say, girls,' Mr Fitzfoster said. 'I was extremely impressed with the quality and size of that ruby. I can honestly say I've not come across anything like it in all my years in the precious stone business.'

Molly and Maria glowed with pride. They'd just completed giving their parents a private *Legend of the Lost Rose* tour – with Madame Ruby in tow, of course. She made it her business never to let Mr Fitzfoster out of her sight whenever he visited L'Etoile.

'Oh, Mr Fitzfoster, such a commendation from the world's leading jewellery expert is praise indeed,' she said, her eyes twinkling.

'Always a pleasure, Madame Ruby,' Mr Fitzfoster said firmly shaking her hand as they reached the Bentley. 'And I trust you will take good care of my two most precious jewels as they start their second year at L'Etoile.'

'Why of course, Mr . . .' Madame Ruby began to say, but was interrupted by Molly and Maria throwing their arms around their parents' necks in a *group huddle* kind of way.

'I can't believe the summer's over already!' Maria whispered. 'Thanks for everything Mum and Dad. It's been . . . eventful!'

'Indeed,' Linda Fitzfoster agreed, thinking back to the girls' discovery of a smuggler's cave at Wilton House. 'I can only hope that this term passes without too much mischief or too many stories to tell!'

'We'll try Mum, but it's not as if we go looking for trouble, it just seems to find us!' Molly said.

'That may be true of you, my darling, although I'm not sure we can say the same of your sister. I think she has a nose for adventure!' her mum replied.

'Like a sniffer dog!' Maria said, pretending to sniff the air. And they all burst out laughing.

'See you soon M and D!' Molly called out as their

chauffeur, the ever-obliging Eddie, closed the car door.

'Be good!' Mr Fitzfoster called back through an open window.

'We will!' Molly and Maria answered, fingers crossed behind their backs on the hand they weren't using to wave goodbye.

'I wonder if Sally and Pips have arrived while we've been tour guides!' Molly said as she skipped along the Garland corridor to their new room, which was on the second year corridor directly above their old one.

'They must be here by now, it's almost time for supper and we haven't ev . . .'

Crash!

Maria, not looking where she was going, had slammed straight into Miss Coates, the Garland house mistress and narrowly missed wiping out two new students who were with her.

'Eeeek! I'm so sorry, Miss Coates! Are you OK?' Maria said.

'Well, you won't see where you're going if you're facing the other way having a chat will you, Maria? As it happens, I'm quite all right this time,' Miss Coates muttered, bending down to pick up the various bits of paperwork which were scattered all over the corridor.

'But I really do wish you Garland girls would slow down and concentrate. This is the second time in the last ten minutes that I've been knocked over by one of you scurrying around like ants. Sally Sudbury's given me quite a bruise,' she said, rolling up her sleeve to inspect her arm for purple marks.

'Sally's here?' Molly squealed, forgetting all about Miss Coates and the two new girls. 'Woohoo!' and then she checked herself. 'So sorry. If you're all right, Miss, may we be please be excused?'

'Yes, yes. Go on with you . . . and DON'T RUN!' Miss Coates called after them, but the twins were already out of earshot.

'Wait, Moll. Did you see those girls Miss Coates was showing around? I've never seen them before – must be newbies from one of the older year groups. They could have been sisters they looked so alike!' Maria said, slightly out of breath.

'Really?' Molly answered. 'Can't say I noticed anything after you decided to play skittles with that poor woman. Maybe we should get her a neon bib to wear or something. I swear we've all got taller since last term . . .'

'Either that or she's shrinking!' said Maria giggling.

Knock, knock!

'Anyone ho-ome?' Molly peeked around the door of their new room – which was, in truth, practically identical to the last one. But the room echoed with emptiness.

'Molly! Don't look so disappointed. Anyone would think you hadn't seen the girls since last term. We were with them only yesterday!'

Just in case you haven't caught up with us over the summer yet, Story-seeker, Molly, Maria, Pippa and Sally had just spent the end of the summer holidays together at the twin's house by the sea, where they saved the day by uncovering a smuggling ring. Is it any wonder their parents were dubious about dropping them off for another potentially adventure-filled term?

'I know but it just won't feel like home until we're all back together,' Molly moaned.

'BOO!' came a shout from the wardrobe as the doors flew open, and Pippa and Sally launched themselves at the twins.

'WAYL?!' Molly shrieked, then burst into giggles.

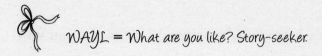 WAYL = What are you like? Story-seeker.

'You nearly gave me a heart attack!' gasped Maria, clutching her chest.

'Ha! Did we really get you?' Pippa said. 'The old tricks are the best.'

'Yes, yes, very funny,' said Maria. 'You know we'll get you back though, right?'

'We'll look forward to it!' Sally said.

'So what's new?' Molly asked as she started the mammoth task of unpacking her many suitcases, all filled with the latest fashions.

'Since yesterday you mean? Not a lot. The bad news is Lucifette is definitely back.'

 Lucifette, aka Lucinda Marciano, was their arch-enemy.

'What, Sal? You've seen her?' asked Maria as she began her equally mammoth task of untangling gadget cables.

'No, I haven't seen her, thank goodness, but I definitely heard her from one of the upstairs windows when I arrived. She was bawling someone out and I have a horrible feeling it was Fashion Faye. Something about a halter-neck strap breaking for a second time even after Faye had fixed it.'

'Oh, don't, I can't bear it. Poor Faye. I'm going to tell her to stop doing anything for Lucifette altogether. It's just not worth the AG!' Molly said.

AG = Aggravation, Story-seeker.

'Has anyone seen Miss Hart . . . I mean, the new Mrs Fuller yet?' Pippa asked, clutching a beautifully wrapped, rectangular object. 'Luckily her wedding present arrived this morning in time for me to collect it from home with the rest of my stuff for school. I can't wait to give it to her.'

'Oooh, what is it?' Sally asked.

'One of my mum's friend is a calligrapher, so I asked her to write out the lyrics of *True Love*, the wedding song I wrote for them, and then Mum got it framed,' Pippa said.

'What a lovely idea, Pips. They'll cherish that forever,' said Molly.

'Not sure if she's back today or not though. Don't you normally go on honeymoon straight after your wedding?' Sally pondered.

'Normally yes, but I remember Mum offering them

our house in Barbados over Christmas as a wedding present, so I'm pretty sure they're going to wait until then. Besides, I can't see Mrs Fuller missing the start of a new school year, can you?' Maria said with a knowing smile.

'Come on, girls. I'm starving! Let's go and see what monstrosity Mackle the Jackal has cooked up for us today,' Pippa said, opening the bedroom door.

'ATYS, baby!' Molly exclaimed.

 ATYS = Anything you say, Story-seeker.

'I've run out of hangers and wardrobe space now anyway. No idea where I'm going to put the rest of it!' she said, frowning at two unopened suitcases by the end of her bed.

'I'll do a deal with you, Moll,' Pippa announced with cheeky glint in her eye. 'You can use my wardrobe space and my hangers if . . . I can borrow a couple of those gorgeous outfits. That blue and white spotty dress is to die for!'

'You're on, Pippa Burrows! I'd say that's a perfectly fair trade. And I totes agree about this dress,' Molly said, flinging it onto Pippa's bed. 'Isn't it divine? You can have first wear for being so accommodating! And there's plenty more to go around don't you worry, Sal,' she went on, suddenly noticing Sally drooling in the direction of a black net skirt. 'What's mine is yours, girls.'

'My favourite words!' Pippa said disappearing down the corridor – her BFF's close behind her.

2

Plenty To Dine Out About

'Daisy! Lara! How are you? How was your summer?' Pippa asked, hugging two of her favourite musicians in the Ivy Room.

'Molly!' Fashion Faye cried as she spotted the twins. 'Wow – I love your skirt, Moll. You'll have to let me borrow it one evening so I can make up a pattern and copy it. Actually, I've bought these amazing leopard print tights which would go with it a treat. I'll drop them in later.'

'Ah, thanks, Faye. Sounds fab! And you look super too. That fringe really suits you. Actually, I'm glad I bumped into you. I wanted have a quick word about Lucifette. Sally said she heard her going ballistic at you earlier . . .'

Maria, who'd been scanning the dining room for anything new or different, suddenly realised how much she'd missed the non-stop din of girly chatter. It felt great to be back.

As she reached for a flapjack, her hand brushed another hand reaching for the same plate.

'Ooops. Sorry!' said the other girl immediately, slightly shy.

Maria thought how pretty the brunette girl was with her green eyes and long hair in plaits.

'No worries, my mistake. You go for it. There'll be a top up tray along in a minute,' Maria said.

It was only when the girl turned away with her tray that she realised it was one of the girls who'd been with Miss Coates earlier in the corridor. *Time to do a little digging after supper,* she thought, *and find out who these newbies are.* Maria liked to have all the facts at all times! In fact, why hadn't she just asked her outright? Might have been nice to introduce herself. But something about that girl threw her off guard, and she just couldn't put her finger on what it was.

Maria Fitzfoster, for the first time in her little life, Story-seeker, felt uneasy and she had no idea why!

'Old Mackle has outdone herself with this cottage pie. It's almost, and I'm scared I might choke if I say it out loud, almost enjoyable!' said Pippa.

'Not sure I feel quite so enthusiastic, Pips, but loving how positive you are. We should all take a leaf out of your book,' Molly said.

Pippa looked happy. And why shouldn't she be? She'd just had the most wonderful summer with her family and best friends and had given the performance of her life at the wedding of the year. She didn't even want to think about the audience of superstars and top music industry people who'd heard her sing yesterday. It had been all she was able to do not to stare at the star-filled front pew the whole time she'd been singing.

'Where's Sally got to? Her cottage pie will be stone cold at this rate,' Maria said, looking around the dining room.

'She went for ketchup . . .' Molly answered through a mouthful of mashed potato.

All of a sudden, the girls were aware of a crowd gathering at the far end of the dining room.

'Sally!' Molly and Maria shouted in unison as they jumped up and raced over to see what was happening.

It was horrible. There was Lucinda, in all her vain, vile glory, her hand clenched around Sally's upper arm, shouting at the top of her voice. Sally looked terrified.

'You're a loser, Sally Sudbury. Your Mum's a loser, your Dad was a loser and if you ever have a child of your own, you can be darn sure it'll be a complete loser too!' Lucinda spat, her face twisted with rage.

'Do you honestly think those twin freaks are really your friends? They feel sorry for you. We all feel sorry for you. And as for gatecrashing that celebrity wedding yesterday - what were you thinking? There's no way you'd have been invited to that. You're desperate . . . disgusting . . . deceitful . . .'

Molly and Maria had broken through to the front of the crowd and were about to launch themselves at Lucinda when they were halted by a stern voice.

'LUCINDA MARCIANO! Unhand that girl at once . . .'

Lucinda, along with everyone else, swung around to see the new Mrs Fuller glaring at her. Maria wasn't sure whose eyes were the wildest. Lucinda looked like a crazy banshee, but Mrs Fuller was so incensed, her eyes had turned to slits.

Lucinda was astounded. She'd picked that exact location in the corner of the dining room to target her ex-playmate, for the very reason that the staff tables were at the opposite end. *Where on earth had Mrs Fuller appeared from? Shouldn't she be on honeymoon or something?*

'MISS MARCIANO. I don't believe you heard me the first time, so in the interests of second chances, I'll tell you again. Unhand Miss Sudbury at once. Never in all my years of teaching have I heard such a spiteful attack. Miss Sudbury was indeed invited to attend my wedding yesterday as was Miss Burrows who performed at the ceremony, not that my guest list is anyone's business but my own,' Helen Fuller said.

The room was completely silent now. Anyone who hadn't noticed the commotion begin had joined the circle of onlookers around Lucinda and Sally. Sally had tears streaming down her face, partly from the pain, partly due to embarrassment. There wasn't a student or teacher present, who didn't just want to run in and scoop her up, but no one dared break the dramatic stand-off between Mrs Fuller and Lucinda Marciano.

'Helen, may I call you Helen?' Lucinda snarled, as she pinched the skin on Sally's arm ever tighter.

'Oh, my gosh, she's totally lost it!' Molly whispered to Maria in shock.

'YOU MOST CERTAINLY MAY NOT,' Mrs Fuller answered angrily.

'Ow,' Sally winced, as Lucinda gripped harder.

'You don't tell me what I can or can't do. I AM A MARCIANO. That's Hollywood royalty, don't you know. If you think I'm going to listen to some small town, *plain Jane* teacher interfering in my business, you're mistaken, lady. Sally belongs to me. I own her. So you can take your pointy, smug, newly-married little nose and point it somewhere else!' Lucinda announced, wildly out of control.

GASP!

The whole room was frozen to the spot waiting to see what might happen next.

'Mrs Mackle, would you be so kind?' Mrs Fuller said at which point Mackle the Jackal appeared from nowhere, and gently prised Lucinda's fingers from Sally's bruised arm.

Well, as gently as a woman with hands like bunches of bananas could, Story-seeker.

Now it was Lucinda's turn to wince.

'Woohoo! Go Mackle!' came an anonymous shriek and everyone else joined in with applause and cheers. Mrs Mackle paused for a moment, loving the unfamiliar feeling of popularity. *Perhaps it did pay to be nice after all?* she thought.

Mrs Fuller raised her hand for calm. 'Nurse Payne, perhaps you might take Sally down to the sick bay for a moment's calm and some arnica to heal any bruising. I fear she may be in shock.' Then she looked to where Lucinda, who seemed to have come back down to earth from *Planet Lunatic*, stood motionless, as an animal might if it was being held by the scruff of the neck.

'Thank you, Mrs Mackle. Would you escort Miss Marciano to the headmistress's office and let her know I'll be up shortly.'

Mrs Fuller turned to the rest of the room.

'L'Etoilettes, I'm sure that you are all reeling from what has just occurred in this dining room. But I would like to request that, out of respect for Miss Sudbury, you don't spend the entire term gossiping about it. Please continue with your supper and get a good night's sleep so that you're fresh for the new school year tomorrow. I pray that none of us have to experience anything like this, ever again.'

Everyone nodded in silence, eyes fixed on her as she left the room. As soon as the door closed behind her, there was an almighty explosion of chatter. Gaggles of girls huddled together no matter what year group they were in, united in their disgust at one of the most horrendous scenes they'd ever witnessed.

'I don't even have any words for what just happened. What on earth possessed Lucifette to react like that? She's lost the plot!' Pippa said, incredulous.

'I don't even want to speak that wicked girl's name,' Molly said, her eyes brimming with tears. 'Poor Sally. I can't bear it. I'm going straight to the sick bay. She'll be desperate to see us. I expect she's just running all those awful things Lucifette said to her over and over in her head.'

'There's only one logical explanation for it,' Maria said, wracking her brains to understand how or why Lucinda would have decided to turn on Mrs Fuller. It didn't take a rocket scientist to work out why she'd flipped her lid at Sally – that was pure jealousy. Lucinda was simply green with envy at the life Sally had away from her.

'She's having a nervous breakdown. That's got to be it. Lucifette's vile, but she's not dumb. If she'd been her normal self, she'd have thought up some lie to tell Mrs Fuller about what was actually happening. Sally was so terrified, she would have gone along with whatever Lucifette said to cover up the truth.'

'I couldn't believe what I was hearing! Still can't. Not just what she said to Sally but all those horrible things she said to Mrs Fuller,' Pippa said, wondering if the words 'plain Jane' were echoing around her favourite teacher's head.

'Well, one thing's for sure – she's for it now – and about time. She's got away with too much for too long. Remember the time she tried to pinch your song last Christmas, Pippa; then when that horror-hog, her BFF Lavinia Wright tried to frame you for cheating in exams. She came through that unscathed – but we all know she was up to her neck in that scam. It's about time she had her come-uppance,' Nancy Althorpe said.

Maria looked touched that Nancy had remembered.

'Do you think she'll be expelled?' Betsy Harris asked hopefully.

'If she's not escorted straight off the premises, I'm writing to the board of governors myself! What sort of message would that send to the rest of the school if they don't expel her? Hey girls, you can say what you want, to who you want – oh, and do exactly as you want – and you won't get into trouble? I don't think so, somehow,' Maria said.

'I'm with you, Mimi,' Molly answered. 'She's probably up there right now being given her marching orders. Come on – if you've finished, let's go and get Sally. She'll be beside herself.'

And with that, Molly, Maria and Pippa ran off to rescue their friend and take her back to their dorm for a big cuddle and an even bigger slice of Maggie Sudbury's (Sally's mum) famous chocolate cake.

3

Good Riddance To Bad Rubbish

'As much as it pains me to lose such a promising student, Lucinda, you have left me no choice in the matter,' Madame Ruby said gravely. 'The school rules clearly state that no bullying of any kind will be tolerated and, in such a severe case as this, where you have not only victimised a fellow student, but a member of the staff as well, my only option is to expel you from L'Etoile with immediate effect.'

Half expecting Lucinda to fall to her knees and beg for forgiveness, both Madame Ruby and Mrs Fuller were somewhat surprised when she didn't.

'Well, Lucinda? Have you anything to say for

yourself?' Mrs Fuller said, still reeling from the way she'd been spoken to.

'What is there to say? You've already made your decision. It's a relief to be outta this dump. Hollywood will rescue me as it always does and you will be merely a bad and distant memory,' Lucinda said with a *couldn't-care-less-what-you-think* look on her face.

Madame Ruby's face on the other hand was a picture. She too had never been spoken to in such an insolent manner and had the girl standing before her not been the daughter of the great Blue and Serafina Marciano, she might have unleashed her fury. Instead she chose to completely ignore Lucinda's outburst.

'Mrs Fuller, would you be so kind as to escort Lucinda to her room, where she shall pack her things. She can wait there until I've spoken to her parents and made arrangements.'

Lucinda looked horrified. If she was going to leave L'Etoile, it would be on *her* terms, not Old Ruby's. *Quick think!* She said over and over to herself. Suddenly she had an idea . . . Well, the beginning of one, anyway.

'You'll have no chance getting hold of Mum and Dad today. They're filming.'

Madame Ruby was secretly devastated at the

thought she might have just lost her only opportunity to be invited to a Hollywood film set in the future.

'Daddy's PA, Elodie, flew over with me yesterday. She's taking a week's holiday in London so she'll still be here. You should contact her . . . tell her the holiday's cancelled!' Lucinda snarled.

Madame Ruby looked at Mrs Fuller expectantly, as though she was waiting for her to reel Elodie's number off from memory.

'Yes, I have Miss Wyatt's number in the office. I'll pop and get it en route to Garland. Come along, Lucinda,' Mrs Fuller said, briskly.

'She won't answer *that* phone,' Lucinda said, a plan beginning to form in her wicked little mind.

'I beg your pardon?' Mrs Fuller said.

'I said she won't be on that phone. The number you have is her American number. She bought a new pay-as-you-go UK mobile at the airport this morning because she was going to be staying here a whole week. I have the number here,' Lucinda said, pulling her *illegal-during-school-hours* phone from her pocket.

Madame Ruby raised an eyebrow in despair. 'Read it out to me,' she instructed.

Lucinda scrolled through her contacts list and selected the one which read *LUCINDA UK MOBILE*.

'*07770 887431,*' she read out, carefully switching her phone to silent before replacing it in her pocket. *I'm brilliant*, she thought. *If I can just intercept this call, none of my family will ever know I've been excluded!* Now all she had to do was get out of that office and find somewhere away from Mrs Fuller's prying eyes so that she could take the call and pretend to be Elodie when Madame Ruby phoned!

'Good-bye then, Lucinda. And if I may give you one piece of advice. Try to be a more amicable young lady. You'll find life so much easier if you are kind to people,' Madame Ruby said and then continued to busy herself with the mound of papers on her desk as though nothing had happened.

There was a clear and intended silence between Mrs Fuller and Lucinda as they walked the corridors back to Garland. Both were too disgusted with the other to even attempt any conversation. Lucinda however was only too aware that her phone hadn't yet vibrated in her pocket but as soon as it did, she needed to make sure she was near a loo or something to dart in and take the call from Madame Ruby in secret. If only she knew when it was going to come. As luck would have it, she felt her phone vibrate just as they were approaching her room. This was it!

'Mrs Fuller,' she began, suspiciously sweetly. 'I know I've got a lot of thinking to do about my behaviour towards you and Sally. Do you think I could have time alone to get my head together and pack my stuff before I leave?'

Helen Fuller looked at her. Why the sudden remorse when she was so obviously *not* sorry in Madame Ruby's office? But to be honest, she'd had quite enough banter with Miss Marciano for one day, so decided to let her be. What harm could it do to leave her alone for half an hour to pack her things? It wasn't as though Lucinda even shared a room, so there would be no risk of her packing anything that didn't belong to her.

'Fine. But you are not, under any circumstances, to leave your room. Is that clear, Lucinda?' she said. 'I'll wait for you here and make some calls,' she continued, perching on the window-seat opposite.

'Thanks!' Lucinda shouted before slamming the door and answering her phone in the nick of time.

'Miss Wyatt?' came a familiar voice through the receiver.

By this time, Lucinda had barricaded herself in her

♥ 24 ♥

en-suite bathroom to make doubly sure she wasn't overheard.

'Yes, speaking,' she answered abruptly.

'Good evening, Miss Wyatt. This is Madame Ruby speaking, from L'Etoile, School for Stars . . .' the headmistress began.

'Why, hello Madame Ruby. Ah, yes. We met at the girls' auction last term. How may I be of assistance?' *Elodie* (aka Lucinda) asked.

'Indeed we did Miss Wyatt, although, I'm afraid this conversation isn't going to be quite so jolly. I have some very upsetting news regarding Lucinda. I must first tell you that she's quite well, however we had an incident today with another student and a member of my staff which has resulted in my having to exclude Lucinda from L'Etoile, for the most severe case of bullying in the school's history . . .'

As Lucinda listened to Madame Ruby annihilate her, not only concerning today's episode in the dining room, but going back to the Christmas Gala and Tallulah Wright's visit the previous year, she felt numb with anger. Still trying to keep up her impersonation of Elodie, it was as much as she could do just to keep saying, 'I see, Madame,' and 'Absolutely, I quite understand.'

In her heart she was mortified, and it was upsetting to hear someone saying such awful things about her. But in her head, she was outraged and relieved that her parents hadn't taken the call.

'Miss Wyatt?' Madame Ruby enquired after a long silence at the end of the phone.

'Sorry, yes . . . I mean, sorry . . . what were you saying . . . I was, errrm, distracted by an urgent email coming in,' *Elodie* (aka Lucinda) said quickly.

'I was enquiring as to what sort of travel arrangements you can make for Lucinda. It's impossible for her to remain at the school a moment longer you see. Once excluded, it is imperative that the student leaves our premises immediately. Will you be coming to collect her yourself?'

'That won't be necessary,' *Elodie* said. 'I will dispatch one of the Marciano drivers to come and pick her up right away and I'll meet her at the airport. I'll tell Mr and Mrs Marciano what's happened this evening once they're off set. They will be devastated when they hear this news.' Then after a pause she added, 'Thank you for calling, Madame Ruby.'

4

An Icy Welcome

'How are you feeling this morning, Sal?' Molly asked.

'I'm fine!' Sally said, yawning. 'I'm not convinced that the arnica the nurse slathered over my arm is much use though. Look at these bruises!' She rolled up her pyjama sleeve for them to see.

'Wow! It looks like you've dipped a sponge in purple paint and blotted it on the top of each arm. Why, that little witch! What I'd like to do to her!' Pippa said, scowling at the thought of Lucinda.

'Well, look at it this way, if all that's left of Lucifette is a bruise that will fade, that's a good thing, right? Ding dong the witch is dead and all that!' Maria sang.

'Yes, but are you absolutely sure she's gone?'

'Sal, she's one hundred percent outta here!' Maria announced. 'It's over, Sally. It's really over,' she said, and put her arm around Sally's shoulders.

'I can't believe how much has happened already, and technically, the school year hasn't even started yet! Talking of which, we'd better get a groove on or we'll be late for breakfast and that wouldn't do at all!' Molly said, twisting her hair up into a neat little bun.

She couldn't help but think how much cooler they all looked compared to last year. Their old blue and white checked shirts had been replaced by plain navy polo shirts as this was the year when students would start earning achievement badges. Molly was secretly desperate to be voted form prefect by the rest of Alpha later in the term, not just because it would mean she was the most popular, but because the badge she'd get to wear was *ultra fashion*!

'I can't wait to see what old Ruby's got in store for us. I always love the first assembly of the term, where she's finally allowed to let the cat out of the bag. It always happens within the first couple of minutes. She can't resist it,' Pippa said.

'Like when she told us a real live prince was coming to visit, you mean,' Molly said dreamily, remembering when he'd held out his hand to help her up as she tripped on the stage stair.

'Exactly, Moll!' Pippa grinned. 'Now come on!'

'Good morning and welcome, L'Etoilettes, to this, the first day of a new school year,' Madame Ruby began.

'Here she goes . . .' Maria whispered, making all the girls around her giggle.

'Whether you are new students or old, may this coming year be your most productive and successful so far! All you have to remember is that if you focus your minds and work hard, L'Etoile will carry you to wherever you want to go. The only question you need to ask yourselves is *'what is it that I want?'* and then let us help you achieve it. *Reach for the stars L'Etoilettes, Reach for the stars!'* Madame Ruby chanted, and the Kodak Hall erupted into applause.

'And so to the order of the day . . .' the headmistress continued.

'Brace yourselves . . .' Maria said again, quickly falling silent as the new girl in the row in front turned to smile at her.

'I have some very exciting news for all of you. As you know, we are constantly striving to improve

L'Etoile's presence on the world stage, while at the same time nurturing any hidden strengths and talents you girls might have up your sleeves. I am proud to announce that for this Autumn Term, L'Etoile has been twinned with the illustrious Orlov Skating Academy in Moscow, Russia . . .' she paused while a gasp rippled around the hall. Madame Ruby loved a spellbound audience and this was one of the best.

'Here is how it will work . . .' Madame Ruby continued. 'The entire L'Etoile sixth form will travel to Moscow in December to give a variety performance which will count towards their final exam mark. In return, a group of Orlov's best skating tutors will travel to L'Etoile to coach you for a gala extravaganza . . . on ice!'

Once again a wave of excited *ooooh's* and *ahhhh's* spread around the hall.

'Bet you didn't see this one coming!' Pippa whispered to Maria.

'Not a Scooby Doo!' Maria said, dumbfounded. This place never failed to surprise.

'Hush, girls, please,' Madame Ruby commanded. 'I know you're all wondering how all this is going to be possible with the nearest ice rink over fifty miles away. Well, thanks to the proceeds from our unbelievably successful *Legend of the Lost Rose* tours this summer, and a little help from the *Friends of the School Foundation*, L'Etoile now has its very own ice rink by the lake, complete with grandstand seating, audio/visual room and temporary changing facilities.

'And as a gift from Mr Orlov himself, each of you will be fitted for your very own pair of ice skates before the end of the week. Perhaps we'll get some new skating badges made up for the high achievers.'

Everyone in the room was on their feet cheering. What a wonderful thing to look forward to. And such a change from the usual song, dance and drama rehearsals. Madame Ruby might be a pain in many ways but she sure knew how to shake things up a bit!

'Your form tutors will run through the rest of the details when you see them in a moment, L'Etoilettes. All that's left for me to say is *udachi*, which you'll soon learn means "goodbye and good luck" in Russian.' And with that she swooshed around and disappeared through the black curtain.

Form rooms all over the school were buzzing with chatter about everything ice skating; who could and couldn't skate; most exotic places anyone had ice skated; UK world figure skating champions Torvill and Dean; sit spins; triple toe loops and so on. The girls couldn't wait to get started.

'Good morning, 2 Alpha,' said the pretty, dark-haired woman, who Madame Ruby had introduced at assembly, as she entered the classroom. 'As you know, I'm Mrs Williamson and I'll be your form tutor for your second year at L'Etoile.'

'Good . . . mor-ning . . . Mrs Williamson,' the twins chanted with the rest of the class.

'I know I'm a new face at L'Etoile, but with your help, I'll get to grips with the way things work around here pretty quickly,' Mrs Williamson said, smiling.

She had the entire class, including Maria, eating out of her hand.

If only Mackle the Jackal could see this, Story-seeker. An open and closed case of it definitely pays to be nice!

'Lovely! Let's get started then,' Mrs Williamson said, emptying some files onto her desk.

'How nice is she? Molly whispered to Maria. 'And so stylish too!'

'First, there are a couple of second year student alterations,' she began.

Lucinda! Everyone thought.

Suddenly there was a knock at the door.

'Enter!' Mrs Williamson called out briskly, and as she did, Sally's face appeared in the doorway, 'Ah, Miss Sudbury I believe? Perfect timing. I was just about to tell the girls. Please do take a seat.'

Molly thought she might burst with excitement when she saw Sally. She dived over to grab an extra chair to put in between her and Pippa. Mrs Williamson watched with interest, keen to know the dynamic of her class.

'Now,' she said, 'we have two new students joining 2 Beta who you'll meet this afternoon at the ice rink. I'm delighted to be your tutor this year, girls, and hope that you won't hesitate to ask for help or guidance. Let's work together to make this a wonderful term, and an even more wonderful year!'

'Sally! How brill is this? Can't believe you're with us all day now,' Molly said, as Mrs Williamson made her way around the room to get to know the girls individually and to assess their skating experience.

'Just imagine how much more scheming time we'll have, now that we aren't having to spend two hours before bed catching up on what the others have been up to,' Pippa said.

'It's a good result all around, I say,' Maria said. 'Mrs W seems pretty cool too.'

Sally nodded in agreement.

'Bit of a change from old Butter Boots. Can't see us being able to pull the wool over this one's eyes,' Pippa said.

'Hmmm, you might be right there, Pips,' Maria answered. 'Best keep our noses clean for once then, eh?'

But you know and I know, Story-seeker, that was never going to happen.

5

Get Your Skates On

As the new second year students walked down the path to the lake, they passed a gaggle of giddy girls coming the other way.

'They must be the new first year girls,' Sally said.

'Gosh, they look so young, don't they. Or is it that we've matured so much more now that we're second years?' Molly asked, deadly serious.

'Moll, they're only the year below us,' Maria said. 'Mind you, I do sort of know what you mean.'

'One thing's for certain, there's not another duo like the Fitzfoster twins, or a fabulous foursome like us in that year. I don't think there ever will be again do you?' Pippa asked.

'I certainly hope not!' Maria said. 'I like to think of us as *limited editions* – they broke the mould after they made us.'

'I bet Madame Ruby's hoping that too!' said Molly.

'Mr Hart!' Maria called, seeing the school caretaker tending to a flower-bed on the other side of the quad.

Mr Hart waved and smiled at the girls.

'Where's Twinkle?' Sally asked, noticing that their favourite little dog was missing from his master's side. 'Having a Twinkle-snuggle was all I could think about when I was laid up in sick bay.'

'Oh, Sally, I forgot to tell you. When Mrs Fuller popped by to check on you last night she mentioned Twinkle was staying with her Aunt for a while. Apparently she's just moved house and feeling a bit nervous, so Mr Hart said Twinkle could stay and keep her company until she gets used to the place,' Molly said.

'Ah, OK. I guess I'll have to wait then. Hope she comes back before the end of term then,' Sally answered, disappointed.

'Ditto! I know we've only just seen her, but I miss her already!' Molly said. 'Come on, Sal. A bit of ice rink chaos will cheer us up!'

The new ice rink at L'Etoile was nothing short of splendid. The 'Glacier Palace' had been built at the edge of the lake so that it and the woodland behind provided the backdrop for the action on the ice. There was grandstand seating, a series of changing rooms, a control room for all the audio/visual equipment, and a staffroom.

'Oh, my gosh, it's beautiful!' Sofia exclaimed as her eyes travelled around. 'It even looks like Russia - look at the ice-cream swirl turrets decorating the end of each handrail. They're just like the turrets at St Basil's cathedral in Moscow. I went there with Daddy one summer.'

The girls congregated at the side of the rink, peering over and pointing at every detail.

'Those must be the new 2 Beta girls, Mrs W was talking about,' Pippa said, nudging Maria who was busy gossiping with Nancy Althorpe about how to crop the photo she'd just sneakily taken on her phone.

'Where?' Maria said, intrigued.

'Over there,' Nancy said, pointing to a pretty

brunette girl with large green eyes talking to Fashion Faye and Betsy Harris.

Maria couldn't believe it. It was the mystery girl from yesterday!

'They're adorable!' Nancy gushed.

'They?' Maria said, only able to see one new face. Then as if on cue, a second new face appeared. What was most disconcerting was that it was the same face – only with blonde hair and blue eyes!

'Twins?' Maria blurted out. She could have kicked herself for not realising sooner. She'd even said to Molly how the new girls could have been sisters!

'Twins?' Molly said quickly, to rescue her sister from further embarrassment.

'AYKM?'

AYKM = Are you Kidding Me, Story-seeker.

'Wow, I've never met another set of twins in my life. Isn't this exciting, Mimi? Let's go and say hello.'

Maria was in a spin. This had completely thrown her off guard. How could she not have realised? Shouldn't she have some weird twin sensory radar or something?

'They're so cool! Honestly, Maria. You'll love

Danya . . . in fact she reminds me a bit of you,' Belle piped up, not noticing Maria's face turning crimson.

'Yeah – did you hear what she said about L'Etoile being haunted?' Alice Parry said.

'Haunted? What? You mean ghosts?' said Molly.

'That's what she said. When she found out she and Honey were coming here she trawled the internet for every speck of info she could, even hacking into systems she wasn't supposed to, to dig up anything hidden. That's how she found out about the ghost,' Belle said.

'Ooooh, yes. She had all the history,' Alice said. 'Apparently L'Etoile was originally owned by the Wilton family…'

'Yes, yes, I remember that when we were researching the *Legend of the Lost Rose*,' Molly said. 'I thought it was weird that this house had been owned by the Wilton family and our house in Sussex is called Wilton House,' she stopped, suddenly aware she was rambling. 'Sorry Alice, go on . . .'

'Where was I? Oh, yes, Madame Ruby's great grandmother bought this house from Lord Wilton in 1900,' Alice continued. 'Apparently, one night, there was some kind of argument at the house, and the youngest daughter, Emily, ran off into the night.

'The family immediately set out to find her, only to become lost themselves in dense fog – they couldn't see further than their own feet. Too dangerous to continue, they returned to the house to wait for the fog to lift, praying that Emily would find her way home. Sadly her body was found down by the lake next morning. She'd frozen to death.'

The girls gasped.

'Oh, how horrible,' Molly said.

Maria had started to sweat. She felt so furious that this new girl had entered her world and was trying to take away her crown for being the best detective ever.

'Mimi. Did you hear what Alice just said? What do you make of it? Come on, let's go and meet them. I'm desperate to find out more,' and with that, Molly dragged her sister over to where the Sawyers were standing.

'Ooooh, you must be Molly!' the blonde twin exclaimed.

'Yes, I'm Molly, but how did you kn...' Molly answered as the girl hugged her.

'I'm Honey Sawyer and this is Danya,' the blonde twin said, nodding towards her sister. 'The girls have told us all about you two. We've been so desperate to meet you. WATC of two sets of twins in one year?'

'Oh, my goodness, did she just say *WATC*?' Sally whispered to Pippa,

'I can't believe you forgot to mention there were twins in 2 Beta, Sal!' Pippa said.

'I know! I can't either but there's just been so much going on and, to be honest, I completely forgot as soon as I found out I was coming to join you guys in 2 Alpha. It's as though 2 Beta never existed,' Sally said, knowing Maria would definitely be annoyed with her later.

'I tell you what though, just look at Honey and Molly. They could be twins! They even have similar body language,' Pippa said, noting both girls standing with one leg crossed in front of the other as though posing for a photograph.

'Hi,' Danya said to Maria, who was still speechless. 'Great to meet you. I'm Danya, the slightly less emotional one,' she said, nodding to Honey.

Maria was stunned. It was like looking in the mirror and finding a girl with a slightly different face but similar mannerisms.

'Hi . . . I'm Maria . . . and errr . . . likewise . . . on the emotional front, I mean,' she said.

Haunted, my foot, she thought. She'd never uncovered any such information, and she'd been through everything in L'Etoile's history when she was investigating the *Legend of the Lost Rose*. Nor had there been a single sighting of anything remotely ghostly since they joined L'Etoile a whole year ago. *What a load of rubbish. What a fake! She's just attention-seeking, which is no way to start life at a new school and win new friends. Mind you, the others seemed to be lapping it up.* That wouldn't last, she'd make sure of it!

'Awk-ward!' Pippa sang softly in Sally's ear. 'You could cut the atmosphere with a knife.'

'You're not wrong,' Sally said, feeling uneasy.

So while Molly and Honey were like peas in a pod, all lip gloss, hair dos and shoes, it was Maria and Danya who had everyone talking. How is this going to end, Story-seeker?

'Welcome, Ladies,' a gruff voice announced as three skaters glided to where the girls were standing.

'I'm Sergei Orlov Junior, son of the great Sergei Orlov who founded the even greater Orlov Academy in Moscow. But you may call me Coach Skates, as many brilliant skaters have before you.'

The second year students were once again silenced, mesmerised by this man who looked more as though he might be an accountant or a lawyer than a skating coach with his round, metal-rimmed spectacles and long, dark overcoat.

'And these ladies, Natalia and Tatiana, or Nattie and Tattie, are my wonderful assistant coaches. We are here to help you be the best you can be. I know for some of you skating will be a completely new experience but if you open your mind to it, it can become a way of life,' Coach Skates said enthusiastically.

'Now let's begin at the beginning – you'll need ice skates!' And with that, Coach Skates, Nattie and Tattie, began working their way around the group fitting each girl with their very own brand new ice skates.

'I wonder if we can customise these for the Gala?' Fashion Faye asked Autumn as she scrutinised her boots.

'That would be so cool,' Autumn said. 'Although I'm not sure I'll make it as far as the Gala. Let's just say the last time I went skating, the ice and I fell out and I ended up with a twisted ankle and a miserable holiday.'

'Oh, don't,' Faye said. 'I don't mind skating when

it's just a bit of fun, but this whole learn to skate, build a routine and compete on ice thing has got me totally stressed out. I might know my way around a sewing machine, but this is a different kettle of frozen fish!'

Autumn giggled.

While the rest of the year babbled away to each other and the coaches, Maria was wrestling with some very unkind feelings. It's fair to say she'd taken an immediate dislike towards the Sawyer twins. Why hadn't she put two and two together? And why hadn't Sally thought to mention it? Hadn't she taught the girls anything? Information was key. She hated being caught off-guard. Ever.

Honestly though, what were the chances of meeting another set of twins, so strikingly similar to themselves? It just didn't ring true. Even if you discarded their obviously similar physical similarities, like hair colour, eye colour and build, there was the fact that Honey seemed to share all Molly's passion; everything from fashion to abbreviating phrases . . . And then there was Danya. The quieter, more considered sister. Maria could sniff out a no-nonsense intelligent approach to life a mile off. She'd invented it . . . and Danya had it. WATC indeed!

'Quiet ladies, please. If you would gather around,' said Coach Skates, motioning them towards the ice.

'After talking to you all about your skating experience, and hearing your enthusiasm for the sport, I feel very positive about the skating potential we have in this year group. A couple of you have more experience than the others and I wondered if I might ask you both to step on to the ice so that Nattie, Tattie and I can see what we're dealing with.'

Nattie and Tattie skated over to Danya and Honey and led them onto the ice.

'They've got their own skates . . . have you seen?' Maria overheard Betsy say to Lydia. 'They must be good!'

Maria rolled her eyes and was about to make some snide remark to Pippa about them being know-it-alls but Pippa had rushed forward to get the best view with the rest of her year. *Have they all gone completely mad?* Maria thought. *Am I the only one not under the Sawyer's spell?*

All of a sudden, music blasted from the speakers and the second years watched as Danya grabbed Honey's hand and the two girls glided around the rink, landing a perfectly synchronised stag jump, before completing the routine with a beautiful dual sit spin.

The girls and coaches exploded into applause.

'That was amazing!' Sally said in awe. 'Just think, we've lost Lucinda and gained the talented Sawyer sisters. I'd say that's a pretty decent swap, wouldn't you?'

'Double trouble is what it is,' Maria mumbled to herself, her face like thunder. She couldn't bear the way the others couldn't see through Danya.

'Well, I might as well give up now!' Lara said, whistling. 'How are we ever going to reach that standard before the Gala selection in only eight weeks?

'I know, right,' Molly agreed. 'I'm more Bambi on Ice, than *Dancing on Ice*. Aren't I Mimi?'

'Nonsense, Molly! You were quite the little ice queen when we trained at Somerset House last winter,' Maria said, loudly enough for everyone, including the Sawyers to hear.

'Errrm . . .' Molly started to say, completely baffled.

'Don't be modest, Moll. You can seat spin with the best of them,' Maria said.

Molly was baffled. What was Maria on about? They'd never had a skating lesson in their lives. She didn't even know what a *seat spin was!*

'Sit spin,' Danya said, as she stood up from unlacing her boots.

'Exc-uuuse me?' Maria growled, turning around.

'You said seat spin. I think you meant sit spin,' Danya said again but more quietly, wishing she hadn't said anything at all. She hadn't meant anything by it, she just couldn't help but correct a mistake.

'I can only presume that you misheard me . . . Danya . . . everyone knows it's a sit spin,' Maria said, barely able to speak, she was so angry.

And there you have it, Story-seeker, she – Maria – had just been corrected. And she didn't like it one little bit!

'Thank you, girls!' Coach Skates called. 'Until the next time, then. Your rehearsal schedules will be pinned to the noticeboard outside the staff room, as soon as you let one of us know what kind of performance you'd like to work on: solo/duet/group routine etc. But for the moment, *udachi,* and see you next time.'

'Udachi!' they chanted back.

'Talk about saved by the bell,' Pippa said to Molly and Sally, referring to Maria's weird behaviour.

'You don't know the half of it,' Molly said, wondering why Maria had so blatantly lied about them being expert skaters. This wasn't the behaviour of the level-headed, intelligent sister she knew, loved and relied upon. What was going on? She had a feeling it was going to get a whole lot worse before it got better.

6

A Sister's Love

Supper came and went in a flurry of ice skating conversation and as the first day of a new year at L'Etoile drew to a close, the girls made their way to their rooms for a well-earned rest.

'Moll, can I have a quick word,' Maria said as they approached Garland.

'Of course, Mimi. Anything,' Molly said, feeling a bit nervous. She'd thought about nothing else but Maria's odd behaviour that afternoon but had decided to let it pass, in the hope that it might all blow over. 'You two go on, we'll catch up in a minute,' she said to Sally and Pippa who looked worried too.

'Over here,' Maria said, walking over to an empty bench in the quad.

'What is it, Mimi? What's up that you couldn't say in front of our best friends?' Molly asked, already wishing she hadn't started by sounding negative.

'Oh, Moll. You're so sweet and kind. You love everyone and everything, which is why I have to speak to you about those Sawyer girls and hope that you trust my instincts,' Maria said.

'What do you mean, Mimi? What about them? And what was all that nonsense about me and sit spins? We've only been skating a few times in our lives and I spent most of the time on my bottom,' Molly answered.

'Don't worry about that now, Moll. By the time Gala selection day is here, you and I are going to be at a level to rival the great Torvill and Dean, let alone, Honey and Danya Sawyer. I've already emailed Coach Skates with a duet routine idea and given him our training commitment. We're going to have to do an hour or two every night, Moll.

'But mark my words, we will win this selection process and go through to Gala night. There's no way those Sawyer girls are going to take this away from us Fitzfosters. Are you with me?'

Molly couldn't believe what she was hearing. Who was this competitive, desperate, calculated girl and what had she done with Maria?

'Mimi, are you saying you want us to rival Honey and Danya?' Molly asked, never having known Maria to be competitive or jealous in any way. She didn't need to be. She was the best at most things, most of the time, so had never felt threatened by anyone. Something wasn't right!

'Not rival them, Moll . . . beat them!' Maria said. 'We're going to take them down. Those little skating pros won't know what's hit them. Right now, they've no idea what we're capable of . . .'

'Me neither!' Molly said, exasperated.

'Come on, Moll. It'll be great. It'll give us a real focus for the term. Something we can do together and conquer. They won't see us coming until it's too late and by that time, we'll be in the show!'

'Why do you want to win so badly, Maria? What is it about this event over any other that means so much to you? Usually you can't give two hoots about the school shows,' Molly asked, feeling like crying.

'I just don't trust those Sawyer twins. Think about it. It's like they've come here deliberately to turn our world upside down. It's like they've researched every inch of not just L'Etoile but of us personally. Have you noticed how Honey even abbreviates things like you? Molly, she looks more like you than *I* do, for goodness sake!' Maria exclaimed, her eyes wild.

Molly hadn't really thought of it that way, as something sinister. To be perfectly honest, she liked Honey very much. It wasn't often Molly Fitzfoster met a girl she thought she might like to take the odd style and beauty tip from. It was refreshing, not harmful. But perhaps Maria was right and she was being too trusting. Maria had never been wrong before. Never.

'OK, Mimi,' Molly said not knowing what else to do. 'Whatever you think is best. And I'll work harder than ever before to get us where we need to be by selection day.'

Maria hugged her.

'Thanks Moll. I'm right about this, you'll see. I love you, Moll,' she said, relieved to feel her sister was onside again.

But what side was that, Story-seeker and why the need for sides? With Lucinda finally out of the picture, surely it was time for some calm after the storm at L'Etoile? But not so it would seem with Fitzfosters versus Sawyers.

By the end of the first couple of weeks, L'Etoile had turned into an ice-obsessed playground. Everyone had hit their stride and was working with or without partners to create the most impressive routines their technical ability allowed.

Skating wasn't the only thing at the forefront of everyone's minds though. Since Danya's claim that L'Etoile had its very own ghost, L'Etoile had become a hotbed of gossip about supernatural happenings. It seemed as though everyone felt they might have seen, or felt, the ghost at some point. Everyone, that is, except Maria.

'She's done it on purpose to throw everyone else off their game! Mark my words, they know what they're doing with their lies,' Maria said to Molly after overhearing Lydia groaning about her shampoo and bubble-bath being moved from one side of the room to the other, and how it had to be the ghost.

'But what if Danya and Lydia are right, Mimi? I'm surprised you're not running to investigate each *sighting*. I'd have thought this would be right up your street,' Molly answered.

'I only deal with reality, Moll, and this is not real! All they want is for everyone to be too freaked out to rehearse, and so they end up getting selected for the Gala. I'll bet their next move is to dress up in white sheets with the eyes cut out and run around the grounds in the dark shouting *woooooooooo!*'

'Well, how else do you explain my travelling shampoo?' Lydia asked.

'Lydia, has it not occurred to you that one of the others might be playing a joke on you? Winding you up?' Maria said. *What was wrong with these girls?*

Molly shot Lydia a *just-ignore-her* look. Honestly, Maria was getting worse by the minute.

And it wasn't just the skaters who were stressed out. Fashion Faye never had a moment's peace without someone banging her door down with costume ideas or requests.

'Faye this is too much for you!' Molly said as she fumbled her way into Faye's room. Faye's father had, with the school's permission of course, fixed up a washing line-type contraption, which she could lower or raise to the ceiling with a pulley. This was so she'd have somewhere to hang everything. Space was always an issue when dealing with so many outfits.

'You've got to say no – or perhaps talk to Mrs Fuller

about how you can send some of the sewing to be done out of school. It's your creativity and ideas everyone craves. Surely once you've put pen to paper and drawn up the perfect outfit, another seamstress can make it. You're going to burn yourself out.'

'I know, I know. But you know what I'm like, Molly. I can't bear the thought of letting someone else help out, and then the end product being less than perfect,' Faye admitted.

'I get it. It's the old saying isn't it? *If you want something doing properly, do it yourself!*' Molly said.

'Exactamundo. Now, where have I put your outfit and Maria's . . .' Faye said, moving a bag full of feathers to one side.

'Wow! Those feathers are gorgeous. Is anyone using them?' Molly asked.

'Yes,' Faye hesitated, as if unsure whether to tell Molly what they were for. *Oh, what the heck,* she thought. 'They're for Danya and Honey's costumes. They're doing a Swan Lake routine so I'm making them tutus covered in these beautiful white feathers. You know, like when you see it at the Royal Ballet.'

'Oh, my, they are TDF' Molly said.

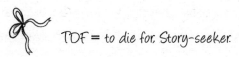 TDF = to die for. Story-seeker.

'You're not . . . not . . .' Faye began.

'Not jealous?' Molly asked, knowing exactly what everyone was saying. 'Of course not, Faye. You know me. It's all so silly really. Just because Maria's decided to throw herself into something, and just because that something means competing with the Sawyer twins, everyone presumes there's a problem.'

'What a relief!' Faye said. 'You guys couldn't possibly have an issue with Honey and Danya. They're such great girls. Everyone loves them as much as they love you two.'

'Thanks, Faye,' Molly said, giving her hand a squeeze and feeling much better at having chatted about it all, even if she hadn't done any of the talking!

Since that night on the bench with Maria, Molly had decided to give Maria the benefit of the doubt, but to build her own opinion of the Sawyers. She'd not even discussed it with Pippa and Sally, even though they were desperate to know what was going on. In her eyes the Sawyer girls hadn't done or said anything to confirm Maria's suspicions so far. They were . . . well . . . perfectly lovely. Molly wasn't as quick to dismiss the idea of a ghost either. She'd seen the research. It was possible after all. Anything's possible.

'Sorry, Faye . . . I drifted off there for a second,'

Molly said. 'Now show me these delicious outfits! There had better be more sequins on them than there are feathers on the Sawyer tutus, and that's not a joke!' she continued, giving Faye a wink.

'Sally and Pippa, you two are a couple of comic geniuses,' Molly said, after she'd watched their slapstick routine during rehearsals. 'It was so funny!'

'Glad you thought so! That third fall I had wasn't at all planned,' Sally said, rubbing her bottom.

'Well on the plus side then, at least you can afford to make a mistake and no one would be any the wiser!' Maria said.

'Good point,' said Pippa said, carefully feeling her bruises. 'I just wish we'd picked a sport where mistakes weren't so painful. I'm black and blue all over and feel like the only thing I've learned since we started skating is that funny bones aren't funny at all when whacked against the ice!'

'Oh, poor Pips,' Molly said. 'Come on. Let's go back, have showers, plaster our faces with mud packs and CO!'

CO = Chill out, Story-seeker.

'Oooh, that sounds divine!' Pippa said.

'Ditto!' Sally joined in.

'But, Moll, weren't we just going to . . .' Maria began.

'No, Mimi, we weren't,' Molly said, a bit snappily. 'I love you to bits and I'm committed to this ice skating thing, you know I am. But honestly, I have blisters on my heels the size of pancakes and I'm done for the night. OK?'

Even Maria knew when she was beaten. 'OK, OK. Face packs all round then!'

'Yay!' Molly said, reverting to her usual sweet tone and running for the door before her sister changed her mind.

'Hey, Maria!' Betsy called over from the ice. 'I thought you were going to stay and watch Autumn and me do our flower fairy routine? We could do with a third pair of eyes on our technique.'

Molly shot Maria a warning *enough's enough* look.

'Ah, sorry, girls. Do you mind if we do it tomorrow? I'm completely exhausted and have some maths homework to finish before I can even think about relaxing tonight,' Maria said, which was in fact, the truth. The rest of the curriculum had paled into insignificance thanks to their gruelling rehearsal schedule.

'OK, no worries,' Autumn said. 'Tomorrow's fine. Sleep well.'

'Why don't you see if Danya and Honey can give you some pointers. They're rehearsing just before you and they look like they learned to skate before they learned to walk,' Sally said and then wished she hadn't seeing Maria give her a death-stare.

'Oooh, good idea. I wonder if they might teach us an impressive spin to include in our routine. Otherwise we'll have no hope of beating them. They're out of this world, aren't they?' Betsy said, watching as Danya leapt through the air into a terrifying death drop spin.

'Let's get out of here,' Maria hissed as she ran off, steam coming from her ears.

'Night!' the remaining three BFF's called out in unison and ran after her to Garland.

'This is getting out of hand,' Sally whispered to Pippa.

'You're not wrong there, Sal. I'm really worried. Maria needs to get a grip. It's ridiculous,' Pippa said.

Molly, overhearing them whispering, felt mortified. What a mess!

7

Ever Get The Feeling You're Being Watched?

'It's such a shame Danya and Honey couldn't stay and help us. I just wanted them to give us a 'wow' move in our routine, like their death drop spin and Molly and Maria's haircutter spin,' Betsy said.

'Can't be helped, Autumn. It's their mum's birthday and they had to hurry back to call her. Anyway, I think we're getting there, don't you?' Autumn said, her nose streaming in the icy cold.'

'True. It's a miracle we've managed to brush up to this standard,' Betsy said. 'You're right. We've done more than enough and I'm really proud of us!'

'Ah, me too. One more time for luck?' Autumn asked.

'Let's do it – but will you come with me to the tech room to restart the music. I hate to admit it but it's suddenly got really dark and I can't help wondering if that flipping ghost is going to jump out and scare me stiff.' Betsy said.

'Don't be daft, Betsy,' Autumn said quickly. 'If there's a ghost at L'Etoile, I'll literally eat my woolly hat!'

Betsy giggled and then suddenly felt silent, her eyes glued to the top row of the grandstand.

'There's someone up there,' she whispered in a panic, grabbing Autumn's arm.

As the two girls watched, an eerie figure in a white dress and bonnet glided along the very top tier of the grandstand, ribbons flowing behind.

Autumn stared, open-mouthed, not able to believe what they'd just seen. 'Oh, Betsy, people don't float . . . it's a . . .'

'I can't breathe!' Betsy said suddenly, tugging at her scarf. 'Don't say it, Autumn, please . . .'

And as the two girls watched the figure disappear from sight, Autumn confirmed their worst fears.

'I think we've just seen Danya's ghost.'

And without a second thought about the fact that they were still in their skates (which would be ruined off the ice) the two terrified girls ran for their lives.

'Whoa, whoa there Autumn! Betsy! What's happened?' Alice Parry said as they nearly mowed her down trying to beat her through the door to Monroe house. 'Are you crazy? What's going on? You've still got your skates on!'

But Autumn and Betsy weren't stopping for anybody, not until they were safely back in their room. They weren't alone, however. Alice had never seen the girls in such a state and had decided to follow them. Within seconds of them closing and locking the bedroom door, there was a stern knock.

'Autumn, Betsy . . . it's only me . . . Alice . . . let me help you,' Alice whispered through the keyhole.

There was no answer.

'Please let me in girls, I'm worried. What's happened?' Alice pleaded.

Finally Alice heard the key turning in the lock and the door opened a crack.

'Are you alone?' Betsy said in a whisper.

'Yes,' Alice answered.

'Come in then, but lock the door behind you,' Autumn said quickly and dived back onto the bed next to Betsy.

Alice was even more worried when she saw their strained faces. 'Oh, my days. What is it?'

Betsy was wrapped up so tightly in her own duvet, you could barely see her frightened little face peeking out. So Autumn did the talking.

'Alice . . . it's the ice rink . . . it's . . . it's. . . haunted,' she said finally.

'Haunted?' Alice asked. She hadn't seen that one coming.

Betsy looked up. 'I . . . I . . . saw her . . . the girl in white. She floated along the top row of seats.'

If the girls weren't clearly terrified, Alice might have thought it was all a joke, but there was no doubting their story. And the fact they'd both seen the ghost meant it had to be real.

'What do we do?' Betsy said, unable to think about anything other than the ghost.

'Look, girls. I'm not really an ideas kinda girl,' Alice said, at a loss. This was all a bit too much for her. *What would Maria Fitzfoster do in this situation?* she thought. *Wait a minute, that's it!*

In truth, Story-seeker, Maria was a bit of a hero to Alice. She always seemed to be at the centre of solving a mystery.

'We need to go and see Maria. She'll know what to do. She always does!' Alice announced, proud of her plan.

'Will you go, Alice? Go to Garland and explain everything. I can't even bear to leave this room. What if the ghost comes to Monroe to find us? Oh, it's too awful!' Betsy said, rambling like a crazy person.

'Oh, would you, Alice? Maria's a great idea. I'll stay with Betsy until you come back. Maybe bring Maria with you and I'll explain it again when she gets here,' Autumn said, not particularly keen to leave the bedroom either.

Alice thought for a moment. This was it, her time to shine. She'd heard and read about all the Fitzfoster adventures and always dreamed of starring with them in some way.

'I'll be right back!' she said. 'Lock the door behind me, and I'll knock once loudly and twice softly when I come back so you know it's me, OK?'

Autumn and Betsy were very impressed. *Go Alice!*

Luckily, the twins, Sally and Pippa were all in their room when Alice arrived, breathless outside their door.

'Quick – shut the tuck box, Sal – it might be Miss Coates coming to check we've tidied up in here,' Molly said, shoving a mountain of clothes under her bed.

'Last time I checked, Miss Coates has her own key and she didn't pant like Twinkle so I wouldn't panic just yet,' Maria said, her powers of deduction as sharp as ever.

'Thank goodness you're all here!' Alice said, as she burst in through the door.

'Alice!' Maria said in surprise.

'What's wrong?' Molly asked.

'It's . . . it's . . . it's the ice rink! Ghost and Betsy have seen an Autumn!' Alice stuttered.

'What?' Maria and Pippa said together.

Smooth, Alice thought wanting the ground to open up. She tried again.

'A ghost . . . Danya's ghost,' she said again. 'It's haunted. Maria, will you come and see Autumn and Betsy and they'll tell you everything.'

Maria, Molly, Pippa and Sally looked at one another and wondered what to do. Only Pippa answered.

'Look, Maria, it can't hurt to go and hear what they've got to say. I wouldn't have believed half the things we've got up to if I hadn't been there myself.'

'Wise words, Miss Burrows, wise words,' Molly said in approval.

'Come on then, Alice. Lead the way,' Maria said, secretly loving the fact that Alice had chosen to come and get her for help. Not a teacher, not an older girl, not blinkin' ghost buster Danya, but her, Maria Fitzfoster, super-sleuth!

'Coat!' Molly said, flinging Maria's coat towards her. 'It's freezing out there!'

'Thanks,' Maria said and disappeared down the corridor with Alice.

'Well, what do you make of all that?' Molly turned to Sally and Pippa.

'Can we think about it tomorrow?' Pippa said. 'I'm exhausted!'

'You're joking aren't you? Mimi will be back in half an hour and have us all up analysing the facts,' Molly giggled.

'Not me, she won't!' Pippa said, twisting some bright yellow ear-plugs into her ears.

'WAYL?' Molly whispered in amusement. But Pippa couldn't hear her.

What was she like indeed?

8

The Ghost

'Maria! What time is it? Have you only just got back?' Molly said, waking up suddenly.

'Go back to sleep, Moll. It's four o'clock in the morning,' Maria said, yawning.

She'd been up all night with the Monroe girls and, to be honest, she still wasn't convinced of anything for sure. One thing was for certain though, whatever it was that the girls had seen, or thought they'd seen, had scared them out of their wits.

The ghost hadn't been about when she and Alice bravely ventured down to the rink at about one o'clock in the morning to investigate for themselves. Maria didn't admit to Alice that she was terrified, any more than Alice admitted it to Maria. The deserted rink was the creepiest place on earth and the two girls stuck together like glue while they combed the grandstand and changing rooms for any ghostly evidence.

They jumped with every creak underfoot, and gasped at every shadow that moved. Never had the wind in the trees outside seem to howl so loudly. At times, when Maria actually thought about it, it seemed ridiculous. What were they doing, tip-toeing around in the middle of the night looking for paranormal activity? They must be mad. There are no such things as ghosts!

Beep beep beep. Beep beep beep! sounded the alarm clock.

'I can't!' Maria groaned having only been in bed for three hours.

'She only got back at four. Can you believe it? Maybe we should tell Miss Coates she's sick,' Molly suggested.

'What! And miss the gossip tornado that's about to hit L'Etoile today?' Maria sprang out of bed. 'You've got to be kidding me! This is the best thing that's happened all term!'

'Why is everyone losing it this year?' Pippa muttered.

'I'm not losing it. Alice and I covered every inch of that rink last night and there was no sign of any ghost,' Maria said.

'You went down there . . . alone . . . in the dark?' Molly gasped imagining what a nervous wreck she'd have been.

'What were you expecting to find?' said Sally, trying to make light of the situation. 'Trails of ghostly slime or something?'

'Ha, ha. Very funny,' Maria said. 'No, there was nothing. But there's no way those Monroe girls will be able to keep this quiet. So ghost or no ghost, this news is going to spread like wild fire, and that Danya Sawyer is going to get the chaos she intended.'

'Are you still saying you think the Sawyers are behind this, Mimi?' Molly said in disbelief.

'I don't know what to think. But she's sure got everyone's attention now, hasn't she? *Danya's ghost* indeed,' Maria said, repeating Alice's words from last night.

'Well at least we'll be able to get more rehearsal time in, if everyone's too scared to go down there now,' Pippa said, in an attempt to get Maria off the subject.

Molly smiled at Pippa. 'Good one, Pips. Come on, let's get to breakfast, we're going to be late!'

L'Etoile was swirling in ghoulish gossip. There's nothing like a school of over a hundred girls to exaggerate a story.

'Have you heard about the ghost…?'
'I heard it was a monster…'
'Isn't it terrifying?'
'I'm never stepping foot on that ice rink again!'
'Me neither!'
'I've asked Dad to come and get me!'

'Blimey, it's worse than I thought,' Maria said as the girls came out of their chemistry lesson later that day. 'Just listen to it!'

'I'm listening to the rumours, but have there been any other actual sightings apart from Betsy and Autumn?' Pippa asked.

'I don't think so, but the third years are convinced now that the ghost was responsible for tying all their skate boot laces together last week,' Charlotte Kissimee said, overhearing their conversation.

'What?' Sally said. 'I've heard stories about ghosts making books fly through the air but never heard of a paranormal practical joker!'

'I'm glad you think it's funny, Sally Sudbury,' Autumn shouted. 'You weren't there. You didn't see!' And she burst into tears.

'Autumn, I'm so sorry. Please don't cry,' Sally said, running after her.

Sally hadn't meant to hurt Autumn's feelings. She was just having a tough time believing any of this.

'You won't believe what I found this morning!' Danya said, as she burst in to the classroom where the rest of them were patiently waiting for Mrs Williamson to arrive. 'Look – it's an old gazette article about Emily Wilton. It supports everything I found out about L'Etoile being haunted. There's even a picture of her.'

The room gasped, everyone scrabbling for a closer look.

'Oh, my stars . . . just look what she's wearing!' Pippa exclaimed. 'She's dressed exactly as the girls described.'

You could have heard a pin drop in the room as the girls peered at a black and white picture of a girl in white petticoats and a bonnet. All Molly could think was that thank goodness Autumn and Betsy weren't there to see it. It just might have tipped them over the edge.

'Just as Betsy said. I feel sick . . . no, I think I'm going to cry!' Heavenly said.

'Where did you get that?' Maria snapped snatching the paper out of Danya's hand. 'And don't tell me it just appeared out of nowhere. Mysteriously perfect timing wouldn't you say, Danya?'

'Errrm . . . it was just pinned to the notice-board outside ice rink staff room this morning,' Danya said innocently. 'Someone must have printed it up and put it there last night.'

'And it would just happen to be you that found it . . . you who started this whole ghost story?' Maria continued. The rest of the room sat in shocked silence. 'And what were you doing down there so early anyway – trying to solve this mystery and seal victory for yourself? For all we know, *you're* behind this whole thing and pinned it on the board!'

Danya's face fell.

'Maria!' Molly called out in despair. Luckily Mrs Williamson entered the room in time to break up the *situation*.

'Take your seats girls, please,' she said abruptly. She was definitely cross about something.

'Maria, I swear, I found it there! I've no idea where it came from,' Danya whispered across the room. 'My research never took me this far – I never saw a photo of Emily Wilton before this morning.'

'So let me get this straight – when the ghost of L'Etoile isn't tying skate laces together, it's taking care of its own press by pinning articles to notice boards. I don't think so somehow . . .'

'Girls!' Mrs Williamson said quite snappily. 'This is exactly the sort of nonsense I've been asked to talk to you about this morning.' The class sat to attention.

'I have just come from a meeting with Madame Ruby. It would appear that thanks to the overactive imagination of a couple of very silly girls, thankfully not from this tutor group, L'Etoile is gripped by a fear of ghosts! I cannot tell you how damaging this sort of gossip and scaremongering is, not only to you as individuals but to . . . MARIA!' she walked over to Maria's desk. 'What can possibly be more important at this moment than listening to me?'

Maria handed Danya's article to Mrs Williamson who quickly skimmed it.

'Where did this come from?' she asked gravely, looking at Maria for an explanation. Danya jumped up to explain.

'I see,' the teacher said. 'And has this been seen by anyone outside this room?'

'I don't think so. I took it off the notice board as soon as I saw it. Although I couldn't say for sure that nobody read it before I did,' Danya answered calmly.

'Fine. Danya, I would like you and your newspaper article to accompany me to Madame Ruby's office. She'll need to deal with this as soon as possible. While we're gone, the rest of you can make a start on chapters seven and eight of Charles Dickens's *Great Expectations* – and not a word of this to anyone outside these four walls. Is that understood?' she instructed. 'Not a word.'

The class nodded.

'Mrs Williamson … sorry … excuse me … I think it might be a bit late for that,' Heavenly Smith called out. Her *illegal-in-school-hours* phone had been buzzing in her pocket since she'd come into the room. Seizing her chance to turn it off, she was surprised to see she had about twenty messages from various L'Etoile students about the newspaper article! Someone had taken a photo of it and put it on the school's intranet, where it had gone viral in seconds.

'Oh, dear. Let's go, Danya,' Mrs Williamson said hurriedly.

The next couple of days were absolutely horrendous. Students too frightened to go anywhere, teachers irritated at having their timetables turned upside down first by extra ice skating training, and then having to reschedule for those students who had chosen to opt out of skating.

Madame Ruby was working around the clock, fending off calls from concerned parents all over the world and, more worryingly, the press. She'd even had to tell Mr Hart to chase away a group of paranormal activity hunters who'd vaulted the school gates with their weird ghost gauges and other contraptions.

L'Etoile had become a circus, and all because of something two giddy girls thought they saw and the appearance of an ancient newspaper clipping, which seemed to back their story up.

For the first time in her life, Madame Ruby was beginning to wonder whether she'd made the wrong decision to collaborate with the Orlov Academy. The subsequent drama that had followed could destroy the reputation of the whole school if she wasn't careful. She didn't know which way to turn.

Time to call it a day and get to bed before the phone rings again, she thought! Madame Ruby turned out the light and moved over to the window as she always did to close the curtains. And then she saw it. A white figure in a dress and bonnet, long ribbons billowing behind as it glided over the lawn towards the lake. Madame Ruby froze to the spot.

Suddenly, she heard a scream and jumped out of her skin. It had come from the direction of Monroe, the boarding house closest to the lake. What should she do? Now that she'd actually seen the ghost with her own eyes.

And from that scream, she hadn't been the only one.

By midday, five sets of parents had come to collect their girls and take them home; threatening to withdraw their daughters completely if something wasn't *done* about the situation. The girls were mainly first years, but Betsy Harris had also been among them. The whole thing had just become too much for her to take, and she needed to get as far away from school as possible. Even if that meant leaving her best friends!

Madame Ruby called an emergency assembly in the Kodak Hall.

'My dear L'Etoilettes and ever-faithful teaching staff. I have no desire to add fuel to the fire regarding the *rumoured* ghost at L'Etoile, so I'll be brief. I understand why some of you do not wish to continue with your skating training, and I want to reassure you that there are plenty of other subjects for you to select in its place.' She paused to assess the mood of her audience. It was about seventy percent terrified and thirty percent *I don't believe in ghosts. Little did they know,* she thought, overwhelmed by the guilt of not confessing to her sighting of L'Etoile's very own ghost.

'But for those of you who still wish to be considered for the Gala, I have decided to bring selection day forward by a week to this Friday.'

There was a groan from the tough thirty percent.

'I know this means you may not feel prepared enough to audition, but that will be taken into account. Once Coach Skates, his team and I have selected the winning performers from each year group, they will be able to focus solidly on those five acts over the next fortnight to help them polish their routines so that they sparkle at the Gala . . .'

'And so she can limit and monitor the amount of people in and out of the haunted ice rink!' Maria whispered to Pippa.

'You've all been terribly strong and I thank you for that. This will pass and we at L'Etoile will come out the other side shining more brightly than ever. Thank you.' And with that she left the stage, although without her usual *swoosh*.

'Is it me, or did she seem really worried?' Fashion Faye said to Sally.

'Yep!' Sally said. 'I don't even want to think about what that might mean!'

9

The Show Must Go On

By Friday afternoon, the Glacier Palace was like *(forgive the pun, Story-seeker)* a ghost town! Having been officially given the option to drop skating completely, the majority of students had chosen to do so, even if it did mean spending more time in history and maths lessons!

Maria, who was on a mission to perfect their routine and win, had managed to persuade Molly to audition, reminding her that Fashion Faye had worked so hard on their outfits and would be devastated if they didn't use them. Danya and Honey Sawyer were also still auditioning with their Swan Lake routine, Heavenly and Belle with their Flower Fairy piece and Pippa and

Sally had decided to audition, *for a laugh*. They knew their slapstick routine wasn't anywhere near good enough to compete with the Fitzfoster twins, or the Sawyer twins, but they wanted to have a go anyway.

As Molly tightened up her boots, she couldn't wait for it to be over so she could have her sister back. It was crunch time. She and Maria would either win the selection or they'd lose. Either way this silly competition with the Sawyers would be over by the end of the day. The whole ghost thing was stressful enough without feeling as though she'd lost her sister too. Twins were supposed to be inseparable and know exactly what the other was thinking or feeling at all times, but for the first time in their lives, Molly just didn't get Maria at all.

'Well done Belle and Heavenly,' Maria said warmly as the two girls finished their routine. 'You did really well.'

'No we didn't,' Belle answered. 'We were like a couple of snails on that ice, never mind flower fairies. I just couldn't relax. I kept thinking the ghost was about to appear any second and cause an accident, so I wanted to keep it slow.'

'Did it look completely ridiculous?' Heavenly asked, placing some pink plastic guards on her skates.

'Not at all,' Pippa said. 'It looked . . . considered,' she added, searching for a word which was truthful but not offensive.

'Don't worry you two. We're up next and watching us will make you feel better. Our routine is a disaster from start to finish!' Sally said.

'Oh, thanks very much!' Pippa faked annoyance. 'Come on then my disastrous friend. Just try not to knock me over.'

Sally and Pippa took to the ice and they didn't disappoint! Two and a half minutes of having the whole grandstand in absolute stitches, the girls glided to the side looking very red-faced.

'I don't even want to look at Coach Skates' and Madame Ruby's reaction!' Pippa said, staring at the ice. 'Was it as bad as it felt?' she asked the twins.

'Worse!' Molly said with a giggle. 'But pure genius at the same time! I actually think the ice looks shinier since you spent the whole routine polishing it with your bottoms!'

'Oh, nooo,' Sally groaned. 'The routine was meant to be funny, but the audience was meant to be laughing with us, not at us! I think I actually saw Coach Skates shaking his head in despair.'

'Oh, well, at least we never have to put ourselves

through that humiliation again, Sal. And on the plus side, we didn't break anything and we've passed the module just for showing up and giving it a go!' Pippa said.

'You hope!' Sally said. 'They might disqualify us totally after that performance and make us sit maths and higher maths in punishment!'

'We're up next, Moll. You ready?' Maria asked her sister.

'As ready as I'll ever be, Mimi,' Molly answered, stepping onto the ice and saying a little prayer.

'Good luck you two,' Danya called as they took their positions.

'Thanks, Dan,' Molly called back as Maria shot her an evil glare.

As the first few bars of *Let it Snow* filled the ice rink, Maria and Molly glided into their routine with such grace and poise, the audience watched in awe.

'Oh, my goodness, they're amazing!' Heavenly whispered in Belle's ear.

'Puts us to shame. How did they get so good so fast?' Belle asked, mystified. 'Must have been those Somerset House lessons.'

'Or Maria cracking the whip!' Pippa whispered to Sally.

'Oooh,' went the crowd as they completed their perfectly synchronised haircutter spin to end the routine, and then they burst into applause. Even Tattie and Nattie were on their feet, whooping.

Molly felt like she'd just had an out of body experience. Now that it was over, she almost couldn't remember doing it! But she needn't have worried. Their performance was a triumph. Faultless, in fact.

'Oh, Molly, I'm so proud of you . . . of us. Well done!' Maria said, scooping Molly to her feet.

'I can't believe we did it! We've never done such a clean routine in rehearsal,' Molly said, suddenly feeling amazing.

'Some things are just meant to be. And today was our moment, Molly. Thanks for working so hard. I know it's been tough but you didn't let me down,' Maria said, giving her a hug. 'Let's just hope the Sawyers screw up!' she went on. And just like that, Molly felt miserable again. Nothing had changed. Not even after that performance.

Danya and Honey took their positions and as Tchaikovsky's Swan Lake waltz played the pair whizzed beautifully and effortlessly across the ice. Split jump followed stag jump, followed camel spin and so many other moves, that even Tattie and Nattie missed a couple. The audience was in raptures.

Suddenly, Honey's toe pick appeared to stick in the ice and she tripped, crashing to the ice with such a thud. A scream was heard from the grandstand.

'Yessss!' Maria hissed to Molly realising that their completely faultless performance meant they had to win the selection.

Molly was horrified. Everyone around, who'd heard Maria was horrified too and ran to see what they could do to help.

Honey lay motionless on the ice, Danya in tears behind her as Tattie and Nattie skated over carrying a stretcher.

'Coach Skates, how bad is she?' Mrs Fuller called from the side. 'I've phoned an ambulance and they've said not to move her until they get here.'

'We have to get her off the ice, Helen, or she'll get frost-bite and maybe even go into shock. Trust me, Natalia and Tatiana have done this a million times,' Coach Skates reassured her, convinced he was more experienced with skating accidents than rural British paramedics.

'Do as he says,' Madame Ruby came up behind Mrs Fuller. 'We can't afford to make the wrong move here, not after . . . well, after everything.'

Honey cried out in pain as the coaches tried to move her right leg to lift her off the ice.

'I think it's broken,' Coach Skates said. 'But don't worry, girls. She'll live,'

'I should flipping well hope so!' Danya exploded, not leaving Honey's side.

Suddenly there was a scream from Belle Brown who stood pointing up to the top level of the grandstand. And there, hovering over the scene as though it was a puppeteer working puppets was the ghost in white.

More screams, as everyone saw it. Before anyone could move, it was gone. The place went crazy. Staff and students alike running around like headless chickens trying to get as far away as possible.

'It's cursed! Did you see that? It's cursed! The ghost made Honey fall! She was controlling it all from above. Did you see? Did you see?' came cries from everywhere.

Only Mrs Fuller and Coach Skates kept their heads as they escorted Honey to the ambulance. Thankfully

Danya and Honey were too caught up in Honey's accident to notice the ghost.

Only Maria remained, a lone figure still in her seat.

You wouldn't be alone in thinking, Story-seeker, that Maria might have shot up to the top tier after the ghost to investigate. But the fact is, she'd been completely floored by what had just happened.

Since the very first mention of the ghost, she'd been absolutely convinced that the Sawyers had been behind it, but now it couldn't have been clearer that they weren't. It was as if the clouds had suddenly parted and the realisation of how unnecessarily awful she'd been, rained down on her. What had she done? She'd been so suspicious, so cruel. She scarcely recognised herself. Poor Honey, poor Danya.

And then she felt a stab of guilt, remembering how she'd cried 'Yessss!' as Honey had fallen. She'd been so obsessed with winning, that she couldn't see what was important. How would she have reacted if it had been Molly on that stretcher and Danya shrieking *yessss!* from the sidelines? That didn't even bear thinking about.

Now here she was, alone, for the first time in her

life having alienated her friends, even her own sister thanks to her stupid jealousy and feeling threatened. How was she ever going to repair the damage and make amends? How was she ever going to get Molly back?

And for the first time in a long time, Story-seeker, Maria Fitzfoster sat and cried her eyes out. Had she not been so distraught, she might have noticed a smirking figure in white looking down at her.

10

Maria Makes Amends

'How's Honey?' Maria asked the girls timidly as soon as she got back to the room at Garland.

'Mimi, if you've come to gloat, I don't want to hear it,' Molly said, understandably furious.

'Molly, please . . .' Maria started, but unable to control the torrent of tears and remorse, she collapsed in a heap on Molly's bed.

'Oh, Mimi!' said Molly, throwing her arms around Maria. 'It's OK. Don't cry. I know you didn't mean it, any of it, you just lost your way, that's all. But we'll help you pull this one around, won't we girls?' Molly said, looking up through her own tears at Pippa and Sally.

'Of course we will! We're best friends forever.

That's what we do!' Pippa said, also collapsing on Molly's bed.

'But I've made such a mess of everything,' Maria said. 'I just don't know what to do to change it.'

Molly never dreamed she'd be so happy to see her sister in such a state. But it was what it signified. It showed that Maria knew she was wrong and wanted to make amends. And Molly was the perfect girl to help her.

'Look, it's going to take some time, and don't forget that Honey will most likely be stuck in her room at Monroe for a while. I heard one of the paramedics say she needed to be treated for shock, never mind her leg, which is probably in plaster by now and strapped up above her head,' Molly said.

'Then how . . . how can I make this better?' Maria said, sobbing again.

'We'll think of something, sis. I'm just glad to have you back. You've been like a stranger this term. Don't go pulling a stunt like that on me again, promise?' Molly said, lifting her sister's red, tear-stained face.

'Promise,' Maria answered.

The next week was pure agony for Maria. It was clear that everyone had decided to give her a wide berth. And the very people she did want to see, i.e. Honey and Danya, were eating, sleeping and studying at Monroe for the time being, with each other for company, until Honey was able to get around comfortably on crutches. She and Molly had sent a big box of chocolates to them via Nancy but not heard anything back.

Gossip about the ghost was rife. Even more students had decided to leave L'Etoile for the term and go home, and Madame Ruby was at her wits' end. Maria had picked up her laptop several times with the intention of doing a little ghostly research, only to put it back down again. She'd been in quite enough bother for one term. For once in her life, she was going to be the model, strait-laced student. She'd study by the book, rehearse by the book and perform by the book!

'Shall we try and get in one more rehearsal before bed, Mimi?' Molly asked Maria over dinner on the evening before the Gala.

'Are you sure? We've already trained so hard and achieved the most amazing level of competency on the ice. I reckon we can take a night off, just this once,' Maria said.

'But it's the last night we can rehearse! This time tomorrow it'll be the Gala and there won't be any more need to train. And besides, I hate to say it, but I kind of love skating!' Molly grinned.

'Well, why didn't you say so!' Maria said, jumping up.

As she turned to go, she ran straight into Danya.

'Danya!' she shrieked, stopping herself from throwing her arms around her and sobbing the words *I'm sorry* into her hair. Molly saw her predicament and rescued her quickly.

'How's Honey doing, Dan? We miss her so much! We miss you both so much!' Molly said softly.

'Thanks, Molly. Yes she's getting there. Mrs Fuller's got her some crutches now so that she can come to the Gala tomorrow. It's so boring hanging out at Monroe all the time. I had to beg Nurse Payne to let me come to the dining room myself and fetch our dinner tonight. She always picks terrible stuff!'

'Did you get the chocolates, Danya?' Maria said, desperate for some approval.

'Yes,' Danya said politely, but looking only at Molly.

Maria couldn't bear it. 'I'm so sorry, Danya.'

Danya looked at her in surprise but still couldn't bring herself to forgive . . . not yet.

'We're fine,' she said awkwardly, and Molly spoke quickly to relieve the strain.

'Well there's plenty more choccies where they came from . . . and some new magazines. Mum's just sent a stash of everything today. We'll get them to you asap,' Molly told her.

'Where are you off to anyway in such a hurry?' Danya asked, softening slightly.

'For one last rehearsal at the rink. I'm a sucker for punishment,' Molly said, winking at Maria.

'If you need a spotter tonight . . . not that you do, your routine's perfect . . . but if you did, I could pop down,' Danya said.

'Sure! We could use all the tips we can get!' Maria said. 'See you down there in half an hour?'

'Great. I could do with getting out of Monroe for some fresh air. See you then,' Danya answered and the trio parted.

'See I told you we'd think of something,' Molly said as the pair skipped off to Garland to change.

'I've got a long way to go yet, but it's a start,' Maria said. 'It's a start.'

11

An Unwelcome Spotter

'It's been nearly an hour since we left the Ivy Room,' Molly said, worried when Danya still wasn't at the ice rink. 'Do you think she just forgot?'

'I don't know what to think. I don't think she would forget,' Maria answered. 'Maybe Honey isn't feeling great or something. Maybe she hasn't really forgiven me. If I had her number, I'd phone and check but . . .'

'But until now, she'd have been the last person on earth whose number you'd have stored in your phone!' Molly replied, looking at Maria sternly.

'I know. I know. You're right. Look, let's get started.

We can just go through it again when she gets here,' Maria suggested, making her way to the tech room to cue up *Let It Snow!*

After a slightly shaky start on Molly's behalf, the twins soon hit their groove, not missing a single turn. Suddenly Molly spotted Danya at the side of the rink, waving wildly trying to get their attention.

'Mimi, stop. It's Danya, something's happened!' she shouted over the music.

But as Maria looked over to Danya, suddenly the rink was plunged into darkness as though there had been a power cut. Then they heard a swooshing noise along the side of the rink.

'Who's there?' Maria shouted, pulling Molly closer to her as they skated towards the sound.

But it was too dark and they were moving too fast and suddenly she lost her grip on Molly's hand. The same swooshing noise came again, only to be followed by a scraping of blades a scream and a crash as Molly hit the ice hard. Then there was silence.

'Moooollllly! Noooooo!' Maria gasped, but she was too scared to move in case she skated into her sister. 'Danya – the lights – you have to try and reboot the power. Can you try?

Then she turned to face the dark. 'It's going to be

all right, Molly. I'm coming,' she said trying to sound as calm as she could. But there was no answer.

It felt like an age listening to Danya scuttle around in the pitch black and wondering whether there would be another swoosh.

'Got it!' she called out and the lights flashed on.

'Oh, Molly!' Maria cried as she zoomed over to where her sister lay on the ice, the right side of her body trapped under the fir tree prop which had toppled over.

'Danya, can you get help? I can't leave her. She's unconscious and freezing.'

Danya ran off into the night without a word. To say she was terrified was an understatement. But to be honest, she felt alive and useful for the first time in ages.

As luck would have it, she ran slap-bang into Mr Hart, who followed her back to the rink, phoning Nurse Payne and his daughter, Mrs Fuller, on the way. Seeing the sight of Molly and Maria so helpless on the ice, made his heart ache and he raced over to grab the roll of red carpet, ready for the Gala next day, and throw it across the ice so they could get across.

'Oh, thank goodness,' Maria said, relieved to see Mr Hart.

'Miss Hart's called an ambulance. How is she?' he said, bending down.

'Well she's conscious now, which she wasn't before so that's got to be a good thing, right?' Maria said, searching for something positive to say.

'She's going to be fine, Maria. I don't think we'd better move this tree until the paramedics get here though. Might do more damage than good if she's broken something,' Mr Hart continued as Molly gave out a whimper. 'I just can't understand it. I strapped that tree up myself and it wasn't going anywhere. It just doesn't make any sense,' he said, scratching his head in confusion.

'They're here!' Danya cried as blue flashing lights flooded through the entrance and two burly paramedics appeared, followed by Mrs Fuller and Nurse Payne.

Within seconds, the group had lifted the tree and freed a very distressed Molly who had suspected multiple fractures in her left arm.

'Are you coming, Maria?' Nurse Payne called from the back of the ambulance, where she was stroking Molly's hair.

'Of course!' Maria shouted back but her eyes were fixed on the conversation between Danya, Mr Hart and Mrs Fuller. From the way they were talking and watching the colour drain from Danya's face, she knew she had to speak to her.

'Just one sec! Dan!' she cried at the top of her voice.

Danya came running over. She was white as a sheet.

'Your face says it all, Danya. It wasn't an accident, was it,' Maria said.

Danya didn't know what to say for the best and she certainly didn't want to wind Maria up any more than she was already. It was more important for her to get to hospital and stay calm for Molly.

'Tell me! Mr Hart said that tree couldn't have come down by itself and you were trying to tell us something just before the lights went out. What was it?' Maria asked, wedging the ambulance door to keep them from closing it.

'It was the ghost, Maria. I saw it as I was coming down the path to meet you. It was gliding along the outside of the rink from the boathouse to the staff entrance . . .' Danya whispered.

'The staff entrance right by the tech desk and mains electricity?' Maria interrupted.

'Yes!' Danya said, the penny beginning to drop.

'Ghosts don't need light switches to cause power cuts and untie stage props. Think about it Danya!

It's not paranormal meddling, it's human sabotage!' Maria exclaimed.

'MA-RIA! If you care about your sister one bit . . .' Nurse Payne screeched from the inside of the ambulance.

'I've got to go! Listen, go and wake Sally and Pippa, tell them everything, then go and check out the boathouse. If you saw it come out of there, that must be where it's hiding in between haunting appearances – and don't be scared! This despicable person is out to ruin the school and almost killed our sisters in the process. We've got to stop them, Dan. Now go!' Maria instructed and no sooner had she slammed the door than the ambulance zoomed off up the driveway.

12

The Hunt Is On

Pippa and Sally had the shock of their lives when Danya almost knocked their door down. By the time she'd finished telling them what had happened, they were beside themselves with worry for Molly, and with nervous excitement for the imminent ghost hunt.

'It just all adds up! I can't believe I didn't realise before. It's this place, the rumours, Honey's accident . . . it's fogged up my brain so I can't even think clearly any more,' Danya groaned.

'Well I'd say you're thinking pretty clearly now!' Sally said.

'I hope so. I could understand it if there had been

previous sightings through the years – if there are such things as ghosts anyway. But I've researched it until I'm blue in the face and there's nothing!'

'Hmmm . . . researching until blue in the face . . . yep, I'd say she's more like Maria than we thought!' Pippa said.

Danya carried on with her analysis of the situation. 'This is a deliberate and planned attack on our school and everyone in it. It's sent the whole place into frenzy. Girls are panicking, parents are panicking, even Madame Ruby is showing signs of strain . . .'

'So what's the plan, Dan?' Pippa demanded, revelling in the old Agent Burrows feeling creeping over her.

'Maria's instinct was to search the boathouse, so unless you girls have a better idea, I say we start there,' Danya said, proud that they were looking to her for leadership.

'Great! That's where we hid to get ready for last year's Christmas Gala!' Pippa answered.

'Why, what happened last year?' Danya asked, incredulous that this sort of thing seemed to happen all the time at L'Etoile.

'Boy, have we got some stories for you, *Dan-with-the-plan* but those are most definitely for another time.

Let's just say we're no strangers to adventure!' Sally said.

'OK, good. Brace yourselves agents, we've a special mission ahead!' Danya giggled.

'She even called us agents! Are you sure you guys aren't quadruplets? The similarities are freaky!' Pippa said with a shiver.

'Ha! No. Now come on. Let's get moving,' Danya was ready for action.

'Hold on a sec, what would Molly and Maria do now?' Sally wondered.

'Easy!' Pippa answered. 'Molly would have us in black assassin gear and Maria would arm us with torches, a camera and a hammer!'

'Let's do it!' Sally said, flinging some black leggings from Molly's chest of drawers in Danya's direction.

'Really?' Danya asked, raising an eyebrow.

'REALLY!' Pippa and Sally shouted back.

'Oh, my stars it's freeeezing out here!' Pippa said, shivering. 'Why do I never think to layer up on these night-time escapades of ours?'

'You'd think our bodies would be used to the cold by now, given that we've spent the last two months skating in a freezer!' Sally whispered back as the girls silently weaved their way through the shadows across the quad.

Beep, beep went Sally's pocket suddenly. It might as well have been a full on fire alarm, the way it echoed around the walls.

'Shhhhh!' Pippa and Danya hissed.

'Soorrry!' Sally hissed back, mortified.

Phones should always be placed on silent during a secret mission, Story-seeker. Rule number one in the Secret Agent's Handbook!

'It's Maria!' Sally whispered honoured that Maria had chosen to text her out of everyone.

The truth was, Story-seeker, Maria knew Sally was the most likely of the bunch not to have put her phone on silent and actually hear the message beep through!

'What did she say? How's Molly?' Pippa asked.

'They're keeping her in for observations as she was quite stressed by the time she got to hospital . . . and . . . oh, no, she's broken her arm!' Sally announced.

'Which one?' Danya asked.

Sally and Pippa just looked at her.

'Does it matter?' Pippa asked her, exasperated.

The ever-practical Danya began to explain. 'It's just if it's the right arm and she's right-handed, that would be so much worse than not breaking your writing arm . . .' But she trailed off when she realised she was on her own with this one. Maria would have got what she meant, she was sure of it.

'I knew it! Another student struck down at the hand of this ghost. Wait until I get my hands on it . . .' Pippa said.

Sally put her hand on Pippa's shoulder to calm her down. 'We've got to find it first, so let's not lose our heads just yet,' she said. 'Maria said she'll be back in half an hour and will meet us back in the room. So what do you want to do – go back and wait for her, or get cracking?'

'Pippa, would you say you know your way around that boat house as well as Maria?' Danya asked.

'Even better than she does, I'd say. I spent the whole day there during last year's Christmas Gala while the twins popped in and out,' Pippa said.

'I vote we go and check it out now. For all we know, staging Molly's accident was the climax of our ghost's performance and it's getting ready to disappear forever. I, for one, don't want to take that risk, do you?' Danya said, fired up.

Sally thought for a moment. 'I'm in,' she said.

'Me too,' Pippa confirmed. 'Follow me, girls!' she said, and disappeared into the shadows.

As the three agents approached the Glacier Palace, it felt eerily deserted. Their hearts were pumping out of their chests, a mixture of fear and adrenalin running through them. Every time they heard an owl twit-twoo or an animal scurrying around in the hedgerow, they jumped out of their skins.

Finally, they reached the boathouse, which was located on the far side of the rink.

'Let's peek through the windows first,' Danya suggested, running up to cup her hands to the glass and have a look.

'Nothing here,' she said. 'It's completely dark on the ground floor. There is an upstairs, and another side to the building, but we'll have to go inside to check that out. You ready?' Pippa asked.

Danya and Sally nodded automatically, not feeling at all ready!

As the girls crept around the building to the entrance, Pippa peeped through the keyhole. 'Basically, the ground floor is split into two sections,' she whispered, lifting the latch after checking the coast was clear. 'This side, which we've been looking at through the windows, is the work-shop side,' she said flashing her torch over the work-benches. 'This is where I hid and got ready last year,' she continued. 'See – plenty of power sockets for all Molly's beauty gadgets!'

'I see,' Danya said, taking it all in. 'And what's through there?' she asked, pointing to a wooden door.

'That's the part which houses the boats. It's open on one side to the lake. It's half covered, half in water, so that they can be repaired under cover,' Pippa said.

Swoosh, came a faint noise from the other side of the door as a shadow appeared to move across the gap underneath.

'Do ghosts swoosh?' Sally asked, in barely a whisper.

Pippa had already switched off her torch. 'This way,' she said, moving towards a staircase. 'Let's hold hands so we don't lose each other. It's so dark in here!'

As they reached the top of the stairs, Sally was too frightened to breathe, let alone talk.

'Ah-choo!' came a sneeze from the other side of the wall.

The three agents gasped. Sally actually thought she might cry.

'Girls – it's in there, something's definitely in there!' she whispered, trying to hold her nerve.

'Sally, don't worry,' Danya said quickly. 'Ghosts don't sneeze!'

'She's right, Sal,' Pippa agreed. 'It's a some*one,* not a some*thing*!'

Danya turned to Pippa. 'How can we see who's in there if we can't risk peeking through the door downstairs to have a look?' she asked.

'I know. And we can't see in from the outside as there are no windows on the land side, and the far side is only accessible from the lake. We'd be seen for sure if we try to go in there,' Pippa answered.

Danya looked desperate. They couldn't give up now, not when they were this close. *All they needed was a way to see down into that room. Wait a minute!* She thought. *That just might be the answer.*

'If we can't see in from the ground up, maybe we can take a look from the roof down!' she whispered, looking up at the rafters.

Pippa thought hard and suddenly remembered

she'd seen a ladder downstairs in the workshop. She tip-toed off to get it.

'Help me put this up, girls,' Pippa said, extending the ladder as high as it would go, as quietly as she could.

'You go first, Danya. We'll hold the bottom steady. Where's that camera, Sally?'

'You sure you don't want to go?' Danya said, secretly desperate to be first up.

'Your idea, you get first peek!' Pippa said, handing her the camera.

'Here goes,' she said, trying to slow her breathing as she climbed the rungs.

To her relief, there was a gap at the top. It was bigger too than it looked from below. Nearly there, just one more step. As her fingers gripped the top of the wall, the gap was just big enough to poke the top half of her head through. As she peered in to the space below, she held her breath, allowing her eyes to adjust to the dim light.

A single candle in the far corner of the room flickered in the breeze coming in from the lake. As her eyes moved from left to right, her hand flew up to her mouth to muffle a gasp. Pippa and Sally jumped.

'What is it?' Sally asked in alarm.

But Danya thought it best not to answer. What she couldn't say was that there, hanging on an old hook was the infamous white dress and bonnet, but there was no ghost in it. She raised the camera to snap some photos, praying that it wouldn't be too dark to see the dress. There was no way she could put the flash on.

Suddenly, she spotted something else. *Of course!* she thought. *Clever! So that's how a human in a white frock can pass for a floating ghost.* As she tried to zoom in even closer than she had for the dress, something happened which nearly made her fall off her perch. A figure had come into view and was walking *(not floating, Story-seeker)* around the dress, as though it was thinking. Danya started to snap away at the figure. This was no ghost, but a girl, with a whitish streak in her hair.

Snapping away she felt the ladder start to wobble.

'Dan!' Pippa whispered. 'I'm not sure how much longer this ladder's going to last – I think you'd better come down.'

Danya took the last few snaps and carefully climbed down before she fell down. There'd been quite enough broken bones at L'Etoile already. All she could think about was the camera, and whether the photos would be good enough to document her story. She couldn't wait to get back to the room and show the girls everything!

13

Special Agent Debrief

'OK . . . spill!' Pippa demanded in a whisper after they'd sneaked back in to their room at Garland.

'Ditto that!' came a voice in the dark, making them all jump.

'Maria!' Sally squealed as she turned on the light.

'Hi, my little spies,' said Maria laughing as she looked her black-clad friends up and down in approval.

'How's Moll?' Pippa asked, taking a seat on Maria's bed.

'She's fine . . . or at least . . . she will be. It was quite a fall but when the tree landed on top of her, that's what broke her arm. It's her left arm at least so at least she can write,' Maria said, much to Danya's delight.

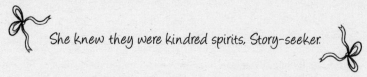

She knew they were kindred spirits, Story-seeker.

'Now what's been happening this end? Have you found out anything?' she said, looking at Pippa for an answer.

Pippa motioned to Danya who popped the memory card out of the camera. *Please let these be half decent,* she prayed.

Within seconds, Maria was downloading about a hundred dark photographs onto her laptop.

'Take a look at the ghost,' Danya said.

'What? You never actually said you saw the ghost!' Sally breathed.

'I couldn't risk speaking in the boathouse and haven't had a chance to tell you anything yet,' Danya replied.

'You did good!' Maria said, placing her hand on Danya's. 'Thank you.' Danya blushed with happiness.

'And you too, my secret agents!' she said to Sally and Pippa. 'Glad to see you dug out the old spy kit for the occasion. I see the Fitzfosters have taught you well!'

'Glad to have you back,' Pippa said, a warm fuzzy feeling drifting over her. 'The *real* you.'

Maria felt ashamed but grateful to feel her friends around her again.

'Now let's see what we've got,' she said, scrolling through the pictures.

'Wait . . . stop . . . oh, my goodness, is that the dress?' Pippa said.

'And the bonnet, yes!' Danya exclaimed. 'See, Sally, no ghost, just fancy dress on a coat hanger. And check out our ghost's footwear in the next shot . . .'

The picture was a bit grainy but the footwear was clear enough.

'Roller-skates!' Maria exclaimed. 'Of course. That's how she got the gliding effect. It would be clever if it hadn't been used for such evil!'

'Keep going,' Danya said, scrutinising the pictures. 'A bit more . . . THERE!'

And there, sure enough, in the gloom was the perfect profile of a young girl with a flash of blonde streaked through her hair.

'LU-CIF-ETTE!' Maria, Pippa and Sally gasped unable to believe their eyes.

'Who?' Danya said, taken aback.

Sally's blood pressure shot through the roof.

'Lucifette – Lucinda Marciano!' she explained. 'The most awful girl you've ever met. I used to live with her . . . it's a long story . . . but she's the one who was excluded at the beginning of term for bullying me. They told us she'd gone!'

Sally looked at Maria for an explanation but Maria was as surprised as the rest of them.

'I can't believe it,' Sally said in complete despair. 'She's been here all this time, terrorising the school. She's even worse than I imagined.'

'Even I didn't see this one coming,' Maria said. 'But maybe if I hadn't been so dumb, I might have worked it out a bit sooner. I can't believe I thought it was *you*,' she said, looking at Danya.

'Me?' Danya answered, shocked.

'Well, not just you. You *and* Honey, actually. Right up until Honey had her accident. It was only then that I realised I was wrong and I just wanted the ground to swallow me up,' Maria said, starting to well up. 'I've been such an idiot. Can you ever forgive me?'

Danya looked thoughtful. She knew Maria had been cold with her and Honey but never imagined she thought *soooo* badly of them.

'Ah, why not. I'm actually quite flattered you thought I had the brains to pull off such a stunt!' she said.

'Are you kidding?' Maria said. 'I've never met someone so like me in my life. And have you seen how similar Molly and Honey are? They're almost the same person!'

'Finally!' Sally said, not understanding at all how two such brainy girls could have been quite so stupid.

'Sorry to interrupt you two new best buddies . . . not that we're not all delighted that you've kissed and made up, but can we get back to the Lucifette situation and work out what we're going to do about it?' Pippa asked scrolling through the last few pictures.

'Hold on a sec . . .' Maria said suddenly. 'Go back . . . there. Do you see what I see?'

Danya, Sally and Pippa devoured the photo with their eyes.

'What is it?' Sally asked.

'That, my darling Sally, is what you might call *game set and match,* Miss Marciano,' Maria said with the biggest smile on her face.

'Now we know what she's going to do tomorrow, and I know just how to blow her out of the water,' she continued.

The girls looked blank.

'Gather round girls . . .' Maria said.

14

An Extra Invitation

'Sit down right now, Molly Fitzfoster,' Sally said, gathering all the pillows she could find to make her friend comfortable. 'I can't believe you managed to talk your mum and dad out of coming to get you. How's the arm?'

'What – and miss all the action? The arm's sore, but I'll live. I'm just gutted I won't be rock-climbing anytime soon,' Molly answered looking forlorn.

Maria, Pippa, Sally and Danya were totally confused.

'Just kidding!' Molly said. 'The only chance you'd get of me rock-climbing is if wearing a harness came into fashion!'

'Ha! Good to see you haven't lost your sense of humour,' Pippa said.

'Listen, Moll. I feel bad, taking your bed. Are you sure you don't mind swapping rooms with me for the next couple of nights?' asked Danya as she unpacked a few things onto Molly's dressing table, which was already overflowing with bottles of nail varnish in every colour imaginable, hairbrushes in all different shapes and sizes and enough toiletries for the entire second year.

'AYKM?'

AYKM = Are you kidding me, Story-seeker

'After what Maria's told me, you girls need to be together without some invalid tagging along. I'm in no fit state to help with the bust this time. Besides, Honey's been stuck in that room with her leg up for ages. We'll be great company for each other,' Molly insisted.

'That, you most definitely will,' Maria said laughing. What she had previously considered as the *Sawyer Threat* she now classed as the *Sawyer Match Made in Heaven.* It was the most uplifting feeling in the world.

'Just one thing, though, Mimi.' If we're out of the

competition, how will you ever have access to the rink tonight to expose Lucifette?' Molly asked, realising her broken arm meant that not only was she out of the competition, but her sister was too.

'Maria's already thought of that. She's asked *me* to take your place. We're hoping Madame Ruby and Mrs Fuller are going to be OK with that,' Danya said.

'You?' Molly said in surprise, not knowing just how much had happened and how far they'd all come since last night.

'Why, Mimi . . . Danya . . . that's amazing! How could they not agree to it? You'll bring the house down!'

'That's our plan anyway,' Maria said, smiling at Danya.

'Oh, no!' Molly groaned. 'I know that look. Don't tell me. For once maybe I am happy to watch this thing play out with none of the usual stress of taking part.'

'Come on, Molly. You walk, and me and Pips will bring your stuff over to Honey's room at Monroe,' Sally said, collecting everything she thought Molly might need. She couldn't believe her luck when Molly didn't criticise her for forgetting something.

The truth was, Story-seeker, that Molly would have been distraught with Sally's choice of items, had she not been going to the room of the only person in the universe who had a better wardrobe than she had! Now that was praise indeed, from Molly Fitzfoster.

'What are we going to do if they say no to us pairing up on the ice tonight?' Danya asked Maria on the way to see Madame Ruby.

'Then we might have to tell her a bit more than I'd like to about our ghostly findings!' Maria answered. 'We simply *have* to be in the show tonight. Mr Hart will have tightened up security around the rink after Molly's accident. If we're not in the show, we won't be able to get in at all today to stop Lucifette.

'The more I think about it, I'm sure that's why she attacked us last night. She didn't want me and Molly anywhere near that ice rink for tonight's show. Which gives us the upper hand. She won't be expecting us to be there. There's no way she'll risk trying to get in or out of the rink today, not when there are so many people around preparing for the show. She's only got one shot at this and won't appear again until tonight. I'm sure of it. That's when we'll make our move.'

'Yes but you haven't finished telling us what our 'move' is exactly,' Danya said, desperate to know the final touches to Maria's grand plan.

'I know, Dan. We always seem to get interrupted at the crucial moment. Sorry . . . ' But then came another interruption, as Madame Ruby and Mrs Fuller appeared at the end of the corridor.

The girls ran up to them.

'Oh, Maria! You gave us quite a shock! One's nerves aren't what they once were,' Madame Ruby sighed. It pained Maria to see her without her sparkle. Even the usually *cool as a cucumber* Mrs Fuller looked stressed.

'Sorry, Madame. We're so pleased we've caught you. We were on our way to your office actually,' said Maria, wondering how truthful she was going to have to be about their new plans for the Gala.

Madame Ruby raised an eyebrow. Students didn't usually visit her office out of choice.

'Oh no, Maria,' Mrs Fuller asked, hoping with all her heart that the Fitzfosters weren't up their old tricks. 'What could you possibly have got involved in since Molly was rushed away in an ambulance. You've barely been back five minutes.'

Mrs Fuller had also been surprised to see Maria with Danya Sawyer. The Sawyer v Fitzfoster feud was as well known to the teachers as it was to the pupils.

'Actually, we're hoping you'll think it's a good thing,' Maria said.

'Yes,' Danya said quickly, thinking that if she did the talking they might not be so suspicious.

Madame Ruby and Mrs Fuller both had raised eyebrows now.

'We wanted to ask you . . .' she paused. 'With Honey and now Molly both being out of action, so to speak, whether you'd mind if Maria and I teamed up to perform a duet as the second year entry for the Gala tonight?'

Maria couldn't help herself. 'It's just that with so much misery around, it would be a shame for the second year not to be represented.'

'Actually, girls, we were thinking about asking Belle and Heavenly if they'd mind stepping in, but if you think you're capable of working together, that would be lovely . . . Do you agree, Madame Ruby?' Mrs Fuller said, pleased to see the girls had managed to grow up and make up.

'By all means,' Madame Ruby answered. 'Mrs Fuller would you let Sergei know that these two are to have priority rehearsal time on the ice today?'

Mrs Fuller nodded.

'Off you go then, girls. I admire your commitment. I just hope you have enough time to do what you need to do before the show,' Madame Ruby said as she went on her way.

'That went well,' Danya said.

'Thanks for jumping in,' Maria answered. 'I think they were so shocked at seeing us the best of friends, they forgot to ask too many questions!'

'They've got bigger things than us to worry about. They're probably wondering if the ghost is going to make an appearance this evening and terrorise the parents and VIP guests,' Danya said.

'Exactly, which is why we need to get our skates on!' Maria said with a grin.

'What are you like?' Danya asked shaking her head.

'I know, couldn't help myself. Let's go and get our stuff . . . and by that I mean Pippa and Sally too. We need to get them into that rink too somehow. I'm just hoping Mr Hart is heading up security, and not some outside company of muscle men.'

'And then will you finish telling us what's

happening?' Danya asked for the umpteenth time that morning.

'Of course!' Maria said.

'I can't believe it, Moll,' Honey said as she munched through the bag of pink and white marshmallows Molly had brought with her. 'What are they going to do then?'

'I've no idea. I didn't hang around to find out. The more important question is how we're going to get you and your leg down to the rink tonight to see it all unfold,' Molly said.

'I just don't think I can use those crutches yet,' Honey said, wincing at the thought of trying to hobble all the way down to the rink.

'We'll have to think of something. Believe me, you won't want to miss this tonight. One thing's for sure, whatever it is Maria's planning, it'll steal the show!' Molly said.

'What do you suggest?'

'I tell you what, leave the transport to me, and you get thinking about what we're going to wear! The morning's nearly over and we haven't even started on our hair yet!' Molly said, trying to remember whether there was still a golf buggy parked outside Mr Hart's cottage. Surely he wouldn't mind if she borrowed it for the night? She only needed one good arm to steer!

'Maria, Danya!' Pippa exclaimed as the girls arrived back. 'How did it go with old Ruby?'

'Done! All we've got to do now is get you two there. Not sure how yet, but it'll come to me,' Maria replied.

'Well, while you think about that, we've had a little idea of our own . . .' Pippa said, grinning at Sally.

'Yep, look!' Sally said and swung Maria's laptop screen around so they could all see:

MARCIANO MAGIC AND MAYHEM HITS LONDON'S LEICESTER SQUARE FOR PREMIERE OF *LADY WOLF*

As Maria and Danya studied the photos of Lucinda's Hollywood royalty parents adorning the red carpet for the release of their latest movie, Pippa went on to explain.

'Can you believe it – they're in London! Or at least they were last night. How about we try to get in touch with them, in an *official L'Etoile* capacity, to invite them to tonight's Gala?'

'But Lucifette's not even meant to be here,' Maria said, confused for a moment.

'No . . . no . . . it's brilliant. I get it!' Danya said, her eyes dancing with excitement. 'It's obvious now that her parents have no idea she's been excluded or she wouldn't still be here haunting the place!'

'I don't know how she did it, but she must have intercepted whatever letter or phone call went out from Madame Ruby so she could stay on in secret and get her revenge,' Sally said.

Maria felt a bit stupid for not realising what the girls were getting at right away, but to be honest she had the rest of the plan on her mind.

'You've got to hand it to the girl. Ten out of ten for cunning. She's pulled off an incredible scam. If it wasn't so horrible, it would be brilliant,' Danya said.

'OK, Pips, it could just work,' Maria said, thoughtfully. 'What better way for Lucifette to get her comeuppance . . . again, than in front of her own parents . . . again! How do we get in touch with them?'

'Already thought of that. And this bit was Molly's idea . . .' Sally said.

'Molly? But I thought she was with Honey.' Maria

said. This whole thing was getting crazier by the second.

'She is,' Pippa said. 'But we came up with this whole plan on the way over to Monroe. Molly suddenly remembered that we had to get everyone's parents' numbers for the auction last year – just in case there were any problems with the prizes. She told me where to find the auction contacts file on your computer and *voila!*'

'All right, clever clogs! I'm starting to feel redundant!' Maria said. 'Now who's going to ring them and pretend to be Mrs Fuller?'

Danya, Pippa and Sally stared at her without blinking.

'I see – not quite out of a job yet then, am I?' Maria said.

As she picked up the phone and dialled the world famous Serafina Marciano, she felt a bit nervous. She almost hoped it would go to answerphone.

'Hello!' came a brusque voice.

'Err, hello, Mrs Marciano,' Maria said, trying her best impression of Mrs Fuller.

'Yeees,' Serafina Marciano drawled into the receiver.

Maria began to explain about the Gala and the school's mortification at not having received an

RSVP from the Marciano's secretary, Elodie Wyatt. Serafina, knowing that they'd been seen in the press in London, thankfully couldn't find an excuse not to be a decent parent and attend her daughter's Gala that evening.

'Maaarvellous!' Maria faked. 'We'll see you around seven fifteen then. Goodbye.'

She exhaled the most enormous breath, her cheeks flushed with nerves.

'Maria, that was brilliant!' Danya praised her.

'I take it they're coming then?' Pippa asked.

'How could they not? Not even the Marcianos could be that dismissive of their daughter, when they're only an hour down the road. It's on girls, it's on!'

'But you do know it starts at seven o'clock don't you? You told her seven fifteen,' Sally said.

'Yes, I know, but that will just be the intro to the show. We don't want anyone else seeing them before the lights go down, or they'll wonder what on earth they're doing there, given that Lucifette was excluded weeks ago. Can't risk them finding that out before she's been caught,' Maria said. 'One of you will have to intercept their arrival and seat them where I tell you to. They'll want the best view in the house for this show!'

Danya was about ready to explode by now. 'Maria! What's the plan? Tell me now or I'm not leaving this room!'

Maria laughed. So Danya had a temper like she did too. Awesome!

'OK, OK! Let's finalise it together!' Maria said, enjoying the eager looks on her friend's faces. She might as well have been wafting a bowl of molten chocolate under their noses.

'So, it all started with this photo you took, Danya,' she began, swinging the screen around again. There, in the dimly-lit picture, the girls could make out the white dress, bonnet and roller-skates.

'I still don't get it!' Sally said, dumbfounded.

'Me neither,' Pippa admitted.

'Look at what's on the table, next to the dress . . .' Maria said, enjoying herself.

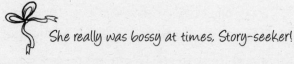

She really was bossy at times, Story-seeker!

'What, that huge, white plastic bottle? It looks like a petrol can,' Sally said.

'No, not petrol, Sally. Its snow fluid,' Pippa said,

remembering having seen similar bottles outside Coach Skates' office. 'You know, for a snow cannon or snow machine . . . come to think of it, I even heard Coach Skates was getting in a snow cannon for the show. But what does this mean for Lucifette? What she's planning? Revving up the machine to cause a blizzard?' Pippa asked.

'You're getting warm. Look again,' Maria said, pointing this time to another, much smaller bottle, sitting beside the drum of snow fluid.

'Oh, my days!' Danya exclaimed, her hand flying to her mouth in horror. 'Is that red dye?'

'Finally!' Maria exclaimed. 'That's her plan. She's going to take her final revenge on Madame Ruby by spraying the entire building and guests in ruby red snow.'

'Only Lucifette could think of that!' Sally gasped. 'It'll be like a massacre! Everything blood-red like that.'

'Don't worry, Sal. That's what we're here for. Time to save the day again, girls – if only so Molly and Honey don't end up with red splattered hair dos and ruined frocks! Those two fashionistas will have been preening and primping since you left them!' Maria said with a giggle. 'You ready?'

'Ready!' her friends exclaimed in unison, and off they trotted to the Glacier Palace for another Gala to remember.

15

So This Is How It's Going To Work…

'Thank goodness Mum and Dad couldn't make it this year. I don't think I'd be so calm if they were here,' Maria said, as she slung her and Danya's costume bags over her shoulder.

'They came last year and you were fine,' Pippa said. 'It was me who was the nervous wreck.'

'Yes, but that's because I was the one doing the *doing* last year. This year, it's impossible for me to be anything other than the mastermind of this whole operation,' Maria said.

'I don't follow,' Pippa said, confused, at which point Sally looked worried.

Eeek, Maria thought. *Forgot to mention that bit.* 'Oh,

no, I'm so sorry. Danya and I will be dancing in the middle of the rink at the crucial *lights up* moment.'

'Riiiight,' Sally said, looking even more perplexed. 'So who is *doing the doing*, as you put it?'

'It's you and me, Sal!' Pippa said, that well-known mix of excitement and fear flowing through her.

'I can't see Lucifette, I just can't,' Sally said, starting to panic.

'Sally, don't worry,' Maria said, going to hug her. 'You won't be anywhere near her, I promise. In fact you're the one who gets to expose the little witch. But from such a distance, you'll struggle to even see her.'

'Promise?' Sally said.

'Promise!' Maria said. 'Pippa's the one doing the dirty work.'

'What?' Pippa said in alarm.

'Would you two just relax? There won't be any surprises – I've got every base cove....' But before Maria could finish, she had the surprise of her life.

Woof! Woof!

'TWINKLE!' The girls shouted at once.

Twinkle was one happy dog. She couldn't believe her ears when she heard Maria's voice floating across the grass.

'Oh, Twinks! We've missed you!' Sally said, sobbing

into her fur. All she could think about after Lucifette had bullied her so badly was having this cuddle with Twinkle to make her feel better.

'Danya, meet Twinkle! She's part of this spy ring too!' Pippa said, patting Twinkle's head. 'It's not a L'Etoile adventure without her, is it girl?'

Woof! Twinkle barked as if to say *you've got that right!*

'Pleased to meet you, Twinkle,' Danya said, giving her a tickle behind the ears.

'TWIN-KLE!' came a voice from across the lawn, as Mr Hart came into view.

'Oh, it's you lot. How are you? I see Twinkle has sniffed you out. I reckon she's missed you as much as you've missed her,' Mr Hart said, smiling.

'Not possible!' Sally said, determined not to let go.

'Mr Hart, I'm glad we ran into you. This is Danya Sawyer.' Maria said, beckoning Danya over. 'We're . . .'

'Yes, yes. I know all about the last minute changes. Just got out of a meeting with Coach Skates. I'd say you have some rehearsing to do, as the two of you haven't skated together before, have you?

'I'll pick it up, hopefully,' Danya said, shaking his hand.

'Mr Hart, there is one thing though. Would you mind if Sally and Pippa stayed with us for the day and evening – to help with the rehearsals. We could do with some tips to make sure we get it right,' Maria asked.

'Sideline tips, eh? Is that what you're dressing it up as these days?' he asked suspiciously. He knew all about these slippery Fitzfoster girls. And their friends.

'Ha! There's no fooling you is there?' Maria smiled, realising it was better to have Mr Hart onside than offside today. Besides, they could do with his help as well as Twinkle's. She just had to convince him not to tell!

'Lead the way, Mr Hart. I might just have a story to share with you after all,' Maria said.

'Absolutely,' Mr Hart said. *Here we go*, he thought.

'Did you tell him?' Pippa asked, when Maria joined them at the side of the rink.

'Yes. I thought we might need some back up. Also told him he'd come out of this having saved the day, which does both us and him a favour. By involving him and Twinkle, no one will know we were even involved. So on paper, we've had the *clean* term we promised Dad, and Mr Hart will be the hero of L'Etoile.' Maria loved it when a plan came together!

'Blimey,' Danya said. 'You girls don't do things by halves, do you?'

'Wait for the adrenalin to really kick in, then you'll know about it,' said Pippa. 'So, what's next, boss. Where's this snow cannon?'

Maria pointed to the lake, and there, on the island, a huge snow cannon rose out of the swirling fog hovering just above the water.

'They must have built the bridge over the lake as part of the ice rink, so they could access the island easily to light up the back drop,' Maria said.

'What, that bridge wasn't there last year?' Danya asked in surprise.

'No,' Sally said. 'None of this was. There was just the boathouse and the lake. I bet Madame Ruby wishes she'd left well alone, all the misery it's brought!'

'It's Lucifette who's brought the misery, not this beautiful rink. I love it!' Maria said, surprising herself. Ice-skating would become her new hobby when her nose wasn't in a gadget.

'So what do you want me to do?' Pippa asked.

'OK. I've just checked with Mr Hart. The snow cannon is due to go off during the final performance, which isn't even a performance as such, more a case of all the cast and crew coming onto the ice to take a bow and have a bit of a sing-along to end the show,' Maria said.

'I see, and because you and Danya are the penultimate performance, you can't go anywhere,' Pippa said.

'How do you know for sure that Lucinda will wait until the last minute to put the red dye into the machine? Why would she take that risk?' Sally asked.

'She has no choice. There's a full dress rehearsal right up until guests start taking their seats. Coach Skates will be testing the snow cannon as part of that rehearsal. It's all done by remote control, so Lucifette will have to leave it working normally until it's been tested,' Maria explained.

'Yes, and there'll be far more crew busying around until the lights have gone down. If she tries to get across in daylight, she'll risk being seen crossing the bridge,' Danya said.

Pippa glanced at the bridge, which looked as if it was rising out of a cloud, the fog beneath was so thick. Then she pictured how scary that scene might be in pitch darkness, and was suddenly terrified. What was she supposed to do, confront Lucifette in the dark? Lucifette, the ghost?

Danya read her mind. 'That's exactly why Maria got Mr Hart and Twinkle involved . . . right, Maria?'

'Hmmm?' Maria answered, plotting in her own little world. 'What? Sorry, yes, Pippa! Absolutely. Mr Hart's going to come with you and Twinkle to the boathouse where you'll need to keep watch until you see Lucifette leave. Then you need to follow her to the bridge. Luckily there's only one way on and off that island, so if you guys and your fierce guard dog are standing at the exit, she's stuffed!' she said, grinning at Twinkle.

'Sounds good to me,' Pippa said, relieved not to be going it alone.

'And me? What will I be doing?' Sally asked.

'Sally, first you'll need to keep a look out for Blue and Serafina Marciano. You know them, so it'll be easy for you to spot them arrive. I'll make sure there are two seats in the VIP section for them. Put them there. We don't want anyone to notice them until Lucifette has been exposed,' Maria said. Everyone but them knew Lucinda had been excluded and would start asking questions as to why they were there when she was *not*.

Sally winced. She had hoped never to see any of the Marcianos ever again, but it seemed she was going to get a full house tonight. Still it would be worth it, and end their involvement in her life once and for all!

'OK, then what do I do?'

'Then, and this is the most important part of the whole bust, we need you to get whoever's in control of the single spotlight away from it and you take over. Use these binoculars to keep visual contact with the cannon, then as soon as Lucifette makes her move to swap the snow fluid, that's when you shine your light right at her, exposing her to the whole audience in the act ,' Maria said, handing Sally a black leather bag with the latest infra-red night vision binoculars.

'I like the sound of that,' Sally said looking up at the lighting deck. 'I just need to think of an excuse to get the real lighting person away.'

'I don't think that'll be a problem, Sally. I believe it's Tattie on lighting and Nattie on sound – or the other way around. Either way, just tell them Coach Skates needs them urgently and they'll drop whatever they're doing,' Danya said.

'Ha! Good one. Thanks, Dan!' Sally said.

'Right, everyone happy? If so, let's get our bottoms on the ice and start practising, Miss Sawyer. We've got about two hours until the dress rehearsal begins and then we'll be off ice until the show starts for real,' Maria said, swallowing hard.

As much as she had confidence in her ability to manage every aspect of an adventure, Story-seeker, there was always room for error. She just hoped that if the worst happened one of the girls would save her, and the school, from disaster!

16

Operation Snow White!

'Sergei, welcome, welcome. It's a pleasure to meet you at last,' Madame Ruby said, draping herself around Sergei Orlov Senior, the founder of the Orlov Academy. He wasn't a tall man, but he was fitter than most his age and his reddened cheeks were scars of years spent in the cold.

'Thank you, Madame Ruby, for your hospitality and kindness. I trust my son and his assistants have been of great service to you and your girls in my absence. My knees are not what they once were, you see,' Sergei said.

'Are any of us, my dear, are any of us?' Madame Ruby agreed. 'At least we may enjoy a peaceful evening watching young, blossoming talent.'

'Peaceful, yes . . . let us hope,' Sergei paused, as though he had something to say but thought better of it. It was clear he had heard about the Glacier Palace haunting and although he didn't believe in ghosts, he wasn't one for hysteria either so hoped the evening would pass without issue.

The grandstand was filling up rapidly. Parents joined staff on the normal tiers, but every time a VIP arrived, they were ushered to the rink-side VIP box and before long it was a mass of the usual international talent scouts, ex-Olympic skaters and even the Russian ambassador. He was, of course, ushered to the seat next to Madame Ruby with Mrs Fuller on the other side, who was sandwiched in by the ambassador's wife.

Sally stood shivering outside the entrance, waiting for the Marcianos to arrive. Everyone else was already in their seats listening to the overture, as it was nearly seven fifteen. Suddenly she saw a commotion moving down the lawn. *Was this them? Was it?* She strained her eyes to see, breathing out plumes of icy air. *No. Hold on a sec, it's . . . it can't be . . .*

But it was. There, being wheeled across the lawn by Nurse Payne in one of the drama department prop wheel-chairs, was Honey Sawyer, with Molly trotting behind with Mackle the Jackal. The plaster casts on Molly's arm and Honey's leg sparkled in the moonlight with glitter and sequins. The girls had matching blonde ringlets down their backs.

Sally couldn't even call over to them she was giggling so much. Bless Nurse Payne and Mackle the Jackal. They must have taken pity on the invalids.

The truth was, Story-seeker, Nurse Payne and Mackle the Jackal had indeed taken pity on the two girls stuck in Monroe and decided, very uncharacteristically, to spread a bit of cheer and become Molly and Honey's fairy godmothers for the evening. However, nothing could have prepared them for what they found when they entered Honey's room. Having expected to find two sad girls, like Cinders in rags, they found instead two glittering Cinderellas, more than ready to go to the ball. Mackle thought they must be psychic, to have both dressed the same. But oh, no, Story-seeker, you know and *we know, that the Cinderella with the broken arm was going to get Cinderella with the broken leg to the ball, with or without their help!*

'Won't you share the joke . . .' came the familiar drawl of Serafina Marciano.

Sally looked up in shock. She'd been so amused by the girls she'd never even noticed her *ex-family* arrive.

'Oh, it's *you!*' Blue said with disgust. 'How are you still here? Seat us!' he ordered.

'It would be my pleasure,' Sally said as sweetly as she could manage, and led them away in the dark to their seats at the back of the VIP box as per Maria's instructions. Instead of feeling overpowered, she felt empowered. The Marcianos were going down. All of them!

Molly had never been so nervous. She wished now that she knew what was about to happen. The suspense was killing her. She hadn't seen hide or hair of Maria or Danya . . . or Pippa for that matter. She only thought she'd seen Sally on the way in but couldn't be sure in the dark.

'Don't worry,' Honey said, squeezing Molly's hand. 'From what you've told me, the girls are more than capable of pulling off a stunt like this.'

'I know. I just wish I could get two seconds with them. Even just to wish Mimi good luck,' Molly said, biting the lip-gloss off her lip.

Honey looked at her new best friend sympathetically. She wasn't used to being without Danya at her side either. The whole thing felt very weird indeed.

'I can't believe they've stuck us all the way out here. Besides not being able to see the rink, I'm practically sitting on the fuse box. This can't be safe!' Molly said, looking at the mass of cables trailing in and out. This must be power central for the whole building. How anyone ever trained to be an electrician, she would never know. It had to be one of the most impossible jobs in the world knowing which cable fed what.

'Oh, Molly. I'm sorry. It's completely my fault, because I have to have my leg elevated, and this is the only place where there's enough room and people can still get past,' Honey said. 'Hey, look, there's Sally. But what's she doing up there? And where's Nattie going?'

Molly immediately snapped out of her *cable* daydream and looked up to where Sally was now sitting in the lighting tower.

'Goodness knows, but if she's taking over from Nattie, it's part of the plan, you can be sure of that. So she's working the spotlight is she? Interesting...' Molly said, scanning the Glacier Palace for anything out of the ordinary, but the lights were already too low to see anything properly. Why, oh why, had she insisted on being a spectator tonight?

Never again, would Molly Fitzfoster be out of the loop, Story-seeker!

Suddenly the music started and the performance began. The opening was breathtaking, the ice, the music, and the setting in front of the rising fog on the lake.

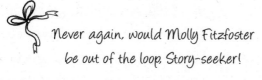
Almost perfect, you might say, Story-seeker. Almost.

17

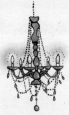

A Glimpse Into The Mind
Of A Ghost

*T*he boathouse was dark and cold.

Lucinda Marciano, dressed in the white dress and bonnet she'd so successfully used to throw L'Etoile into turmoil, stood silently, looking towards the snow cannon on the island. *This was it,* she thought. Her revenge. And how creepy that the same fog which had taken poor Emily Wilton all those years ago, had chosen tonight to come and help her with her plan.

She'd done some pretty spectacular things during her time at L'Etoile, but never something on this scale before . . . something which would affect absolutely everyone. Madame Ruby and her beloved school would never recover from this evening. She couldn't wait to read about it in tomorrow's papers, to scour the photographs and devour all the videos, which would most assuredly be posted online. Lucinda Marciano's revenge would rain down on L'Etoile like no horror they could ever imagine.

She turned towards the Glacier Palace, listening to the audience applaud as year after year sent their best routines onto the ice. It was perfect. Such a beautiful scene. An icy, still night, with the moon and stars lighting up the sky. Only the fog hung like a warning over the water, but they were all too engrossed in its beauty to realise.

Suddenly, she heard it, the familiar opening notes of *Bolero*. The fifth form had created the most incredible group routine to the Torvill and Dean's legendary Olympic gold song. Lucinda had planned everything down to the last second. She should wait until forty seconds into the track and then roller-skate over to the bridge. The audience and crew would be so engrossed, they wouldn't notice her glide across to the snow cannon with the red dye. Then she had one more song to complete her mission before the *Finale* and her own *grand finale*. As she held on for those last few seconds, she couldn't help but smile at how impressive her plotting had been.

After she'd been excluded and bolted to the boathouse for refuge it didn't take her long to work out her revenge. Hanging around close to the school, she kept her nose to the ground for any gossip. As usual there was plenty. Danya and her ghost story provided the perfect backdrop for her to terrorise the school. She just needed to get her facts right and so had asked her father's PA, Elodie Wyatt to dig up anything she could on Emily Wilton and send it through.

Elodie, worried at failing any of the Marciano clan, moved heaven and earth to locate the article with the photo of Emily Wilton in her bonnet, which Lucinda posted on the notice board for the girls to find. All she had to do then was to raid the drama department for a suitable costume and she was set to roam the school and cause havoc.

She'd fooled everyone with her ghostly appearances, and she had to admit the roller-skates were a stroke of brilliance. She could kiss Lavinia Wright for leaving those behind last term! She'd even managed to terrorise those meddling Fitzfoster twins with her tree accident and was only sorry that it hadn't ended in Maria not being able to perform at the Gala, as well as that dumb sister of hers. Still at least they'd both be there for the *main event*.

Everything she'd done so far led to this moment and she was ready for it. When it was done and the Glacier Palace was reeling, she would get into the car she had booked to London to meet stupid Elodie Wyatt, and fly home to her loving parents to talk about going to school in Los Angeles.

It was the perfect plan. The perfect revenge. And no one would ever know the truth.

18

Operation Girl Versus Ghost

'Oh, my gosh, there she is,' Pippa whispered to Mr Hart as they stood quietly in the boathouse shadows. No matter how many times she told herself that it was just Lucinda in that white dress and bonnet, she couldn't help but feel freaked out. *Get a grip, Pippa*, she thought and focused on Mr Hart. 'You're sure the cannon goes off during the finale?'

'Yes,' Mr Hart said, wondering if he'd done the right thing not telling his daughter what was happening. 'I watched the run-through myself this afternoon. Coach Skates is operating the cannon remote control himself. So Lucinda will have to make the swap during Maria and Danya's performance before Coach Skates hits the remote.'

'I just hope Sally's up there with that spotlight and ready to catch Lucifette in the act! If we don't expose her as she's putting the red dye into the cannon, Coach Skates won't know anything's wrong, and might just press the button anyway. In which case we'll have failed our mission completely!' Pippa whispered, also beginning to wonder whether they should have told Mrs Fuller the whole story and had Lucinda arrested or something hours ago. This last minute exposé would have maximum impact. But the closer it got, the riskier it felt!

'I haven't seen a fog like this here for years,' Mr Hart murmured watching it get denser by the second. 'Perfect conditions for anyone who doesn't want to be seen doing something they shouldn't!'

Twinkle gave a little whimper as she sniffed the air.

'Oh, no!' Pippa gasped, as they followed, suddenly realising she could barely see Lucinda ahead of them now through the thick fog. 'Mr Hart! You're right! It's getting even worse! Look at the bridge – we could see the whole thing when we first got down here – now I can only see the hand rail. At this rate, we'll lose sight of Lucifette completely.'

'I'd say that's not our only problem. I can't even see the snow cannon, can you?' Mr Hart said, picking up the pace to get to the bridge before it disappeared.

Pippa sighed. All her fears had come true. If the snow cannon was completely hidden, then Lucinda's sabotage would be too. There would be nothing a million spotlights could pick out, let alone Sally's one, searching the island in the dark.

'Oh, Mr Hart. I need to get to Coach Skates and stop him from setting off the cannon,' Pippa said, starting to turn around, only to realise that she couldn't see her hand in front of her face.

'No, Pippa. We stick together. It's not safe to split up now. The fog might not have reached the rink yet, but we're in the thick of it here,' Mr Hart instructed, looking around him.

'All right, but there's only one thing for it then' Pippa said, breathlessly. 'We're going to have to find Lucifette and that cannon ourselves and somehow disable both! Listen, *Bolero* has just finished, which means we've got the time it takes for Maria and Danya to perform *Let It* Snow before it goes off and the whole place is covered in murderous confetti!'

'Right,' Mr Hart said. 'Then stay close, please. Goodness only knows how we're going to find her, and I'm keen not to lose you in the process and have to send out the dogs to find you!'

'OMG, you're brilliant!' Pippa said almost exploding with relief.

'I am?' Mr Hart asked.

Woof, came the quietest little bark from Twinkle.

Mr Hart smiled. 'Ha! How could I forget, Twinkle? Who needs eyes and ears when you have the best nose in England? Come on girl. Find Lucinda!'

'Ready?' Danya said, squeezing Maria's hand.

'Ready as I'll ever be!' Maria said, feeling completely helpless. She never wanted a walkie-talkie watch as much as she did right now. It wasn't Sally she was worried about. She'd seen the Marcianos take their seats and watched Sally climb up to the spotlight, but she had no idea what was going on with Pippa and Mr H. What if they'd missed Lucinda leaving the boathouse for some reason and weren't there to block the entrance to the bridge?

'Don't worry, Maria. It's all going to go to plan. Come on, let's do this!' Danya said, taking Maria by the hand and gliding onto the ice as Madame Ruby announced their performance.

'Ladies and gentlemen. I hope you will agree that this has been one of the most breathtaking evenings of artistic and technical ability the school has ever hosted. What my L'Etoilettes, under the expert guidance of Sergei and his team, have achieved in one term is simply stunning and this next performance is no exception. Please welcome two girls from the second year who have come together this afternoon no less, against the adversity of losing their original partners to injury, to perform for you. I give you Maria Fitzfoster and Danya Sawyer!'

The crowd was on its feet, cheering and clapping, jollied along by the song's intro.

'Beautiful *toe loop*,' Sergei Orlov gushed to Madame Ruby. 'Wow! Stunning *camel spin*! Madame Ruby glowed with pride.

'Nearly there,' Maria whispered to Danya as they came together on the ice. 'Any second now, Lucifette will get her comeuppance!'

'Hold on, something's wrong!' Danya cried. 'Look at the spotlight!'

The girls glanced up at Sally who was wildly moving the spotlight in circles on the island.

'Oh, no! Look at the fog!' Maria said, feeling frantic, but managing to keep up the routine. 'It's not so bad here yet, but look at the island! You can't even see it! She . . . she . . . can't expose Lucifette . . . she can't even see her!'

'Oh, my days!' Danya squealed, 'She's probably already made the swap! And we've missed her do it!'

Any second now, their song would be over and Coach Skates would hit the remote to activate the snow cannon.

Molly, having leapt out of her seat for a decent rink-side view as soon as the girls had begun their routine, saw the sudden panic in Maria's face. Within seconds, she had managed to climb halfway up the lighting tower, which was no mean feat for someone with only one working arm.

'Sally!' she hissed. What's going on?'

'It's the snow cannon....' Sally said in a panic. 'Lucifette's put red dye in it – it's going to go off any second! I was supposed to light her up in the act so Coach Skates doesn't press the button – but the fog – it's too thick! I can't even see her!'

'OMG!' Molly said under her breath as a round of applause went up for the two exquisite, if a little chatty, skaters who had just finished.

Then, the music for the closing song floated through the ice rink as everyone involved in the Gala, glided onto the ice to take a bow. All of a sudden a whoosh went up on the island and a huge gust of red snow burst forth towards the ice rink.

The audience gasped, seeing the cloud coming towards them, then sighed with relief as the torrent of snow seemed to shoot up to the sky and away towards the other side of the lake as though a gust of wind from nowhere had blown it in the other direction.

'What in the blazes . . ?' Madame Ruby gasped.

Mrs Fuller was up and out of her seat wondering what was happening, but she was so penned in she couldn't get out of the stand.

Molly looked at Maria, who stood open-mouthed on the ice and immediately realised the plan had gone terribly wrong. She had to do something! Then it struck her. The cables! There had to be one leading to the snow cannon. She had to shut it off!

'Molly!' Honey cried, seeing her friend racing towards her. 'What's going on?'

But Molly wasn't listening. She'd spotted a thick black cable leading along the side of the rink and out of the building. That had to be it – the one to the island. *Here goes!* she thought, and pulled the plug from its socket.

There was silence as the whooshing stopped. So

too did the music thanks to Nattie and Tattie on the sound desk.

Molly ran to the side of the rink where Maria and Danya were white.

'It worked!' she squealed, pointing to the island with her good arm. 'I cut the power! I cut the power!'

'Oh, Molly, you clever thing,' Maria said, cuddling her sister. 'I can't believe I didn't have a contingency for fog. What a disaster! Lucifette will be long gone now on those roller-skates. We'll never get her.'

By now, the house lights had gone up and Madame Ruby had grabbed a microphone and made her way to the front of the grandstand.

'Ladies and gentlemen. I'm sure you are all by now very aware, that this isn't the grand finale my staff or I expected, and as soon as we get to the bottom of what exactly happened here this evening, I will provide you all with an explanation,' she said as calmly as she could.

'In the meantime, would you be kind enough to put your hands together for one of the most wonderful Galas L'Etoile has ever seen. If you'd like to make your way to the Ivy room for some refreshments, I will be with you shortly. Thank you, once again, for joining us.'

The grandstand began to clap and cheer their girls. No one could deny the level of talent. It was just the final few minutes which had been slightly odd.

As the rest of the school cleared the rink, Maria, Danya, Molly, Sally and Honey in her drama department wheelchair, huddled at one end of the rink in earnest conversation.

'At least we stopped the snow cannon!' Sally said.

'Yeah, it's great, but it wasn't quite what we'd hoped. I wonder where Lucifette is now. Halfway to the airport, I expect!' Maria whispered as Coach Skates walked past, deep in conference with Sergei Olav, Nattie and Tattie about what might have gone wrong.

'Oh, Maria!' Molly said. 'You did your best. You can't win them all and you and Danya were out of this world on the ice!'

'Thanks, Moll. But I can't help feeling that all we've managed to do is confuse everybody. A term's worth of terror was supposed to evaporate with Lucifette being caught sabotaging the snow machine and revealed to the whole school and her parents, but it didn't go down like that at all!' Maria groaned.

'You can't control the weather, Maria,' Danya said.

'No, but I should have noticed it was getting worse. I . . .' Suddenly she stopped talking, seeing Blue Marciano making a bee-line for poor, confused Madame Ruby.

'MADAME RUBY!' Blue Marciano shouted as the rest of the guests filed out.

His presence hit Madame Ruby like a lightning bolt. What was *he* doing here?

'M . . . M . . . Mr Marciano!' she stammered. 'Mrs Marciano . . .' but before she could speak, Blue Marciano exploded.

'Madame Ruby. My wife and I are without doubt the busiest people on the planet, so you'll forgive me for wondering why we've been called all the way down here to a show our daughter doesn't even feature in!' he bawled.

'I . . .' Madame Ruby began again only to be interrupted for a second time.

'Errr . . . I think I might have an answer for you, Mr Marciano,' came Mrs Fuller's voice from the entrance to the Glacier Palace.

Everyone swung around to look. The sight that followed Mrs Fuller would have been comical if it wasn't so unexpected.

As Helen Fuller stood to one side, there, dripping red liquid was none other than *the ghost* in her stained bonnet and petticoats.

'Lucinda!' Madame Ruby gasped, in unison with Mr and Mrs Marciano.

'Yessss!' Maria hissed in delight. And this time, her friends joined in!

Lucinda stood, staring at the floor, unable to move given that the fiercest-looking Twinkle you'd ever seen still had the bonnet ribbons clenched in her teeth. Behind her stood an even fiercer-looking, red-snow-soaked Mr Hart and a shivering Pippa.

'It would seem, Madame Ruby . . . Mr and Mrs Marciano . . . that Lucinda is our resident *ghost* and was behind the sabotaging of the snow cannon this evening.

Had it not been for the quick thinking and courageous actions of my father and Miss Burrows, the grand finale would have been a *bloodbath*, for want of a more appropriate description,' Mrs Fuller explained.

'Lucinda?' her mother questioned, moving a little closer. To be honest, it could have been anyone under that bonnet given her red-stained face, which now had tear tracks running down it.

'Mamma, I . . .' Lucinda started but was too upset for any words to come out.

This would ordinarily have been a good opportunity for Mrs Marciano to play the *doting mother* role, but as soon as she realised it would involve her getting red dye on her white coat, she took a few steps back.

Lucinda had felt alone for most of her life, but never more so than at that moment. Everyone around her was looking at her with such disgust. She had so thought she'd got away with everything, but now look what had happened. Come to think of it, how were her parents even there anyway? They should have been on a film set somewhere, doing what they do best, leaving their only daughter to fend for herself.

She looked to her Dad for help, but there was nothing in his face which made her feel like she had his support.

'Madame Ruby, I demand an explanation! I feel as though I'm in one of my movies. What is the meaning of this? What are we all doing here in this ridiculous situation?' Mr Marciano bellowed.

'That, Mr Marciano, is the question! Your daughter should no more be on the school premises, than you should!' Madame Ruby exclaimed, furious with Lucinda for all the trouble she had caused.

'What did you say?' Blue Marciano yelled, never having been spoken to in such a manner.

'Go, Ruby!' Molly whispered to the girls.

'The fact of the matter is that I excluded your daughter before the term even began, for the most severe case of bullying ever witnessed at L'Etoile. So you can understand my surprise at seeing all three of you here this evening,' she took a breath. 'I am not yet apprised of all the facts as to how this was kept from you, or exactly what happened on the island this evening, but there is one thing I *am* sure of,' she turned to Lucinda.

'Lucinda Marciano, you are without doubt, the most deceitful, spiteful, *lost* child I have ever met. But is it any wonder given the childhood you have endured with such *busy* parents as yours?'

She glanced at Blue and Serafina Marciano who were open-mouthed with shock, but Madame Ruby hadn't finished yet. She turned back to Lucinda.

'In hiding out at L'Etoile all these weeks, posing as a ghost to terrorise staff and students alike, you have not only broken the laws of this school, but the laws of this country. In ten seconds I will telephone the police to have you arrested for trespassing – among other more serious charges – unless you and your parents have removed yourselves from my property by the time I pick up the phone. I'm sure you are as keen to keep this scandal out of the press as I am?'

There was silence among the onlookers as Blue and Serafina grabbed their only daughter by the petticoats and rollered her away to the car as fast as their legs and her skates would carry them. It was all Maria and friends could do to keep from whooping and cheering their headmistress.

Madame Ruby beckoned them to come closer.

'Girls, would you please find Miss Burrows some towels and take her back to Garland immediately for a warm bath and a hot chocolate. This child is positively freezing!' she said, seeing Pippa's teeth chattering like mad.

The girls didn't need to be asked twice. They were absolutely desperate to gossip about everything that had happened, and departed with Honey, still in her wheelchair, Twinkle in her lap, and Pippa wrapped up like an Egyptian mummy.

'David,' Madame Ruby turned now to Mr Hart, who hadn't even noticed Twinkle disappear with the girls. 'Would you get cleaned up and meet me in my office in ten minutes? I need a complete debrief of what happened on that island before I can work out what to say to the rest of the girls' parents and VIPs waiting in the Ivy Room.

Mr Hart nodded.

'You too, Helen – via checking with security that the Marcianos have indeed left the building!' Madame Ruby said.

'Of course!' Mrs Fuller said and promptly left.

Madame Ruby felt a wave of relief wash over her. There were no such things as ghosts! She knew that. Of course she knew that. And with a nod to Coach Skates and a last look at the Glacier Palace, she swooshed around on her heel and headed for her office.

Thank goodness for that, Story-seeker.
Madame Ruby had got her swoosh back!

19

Operation What Happened On The Island!

'Oh, Pippa! Thank goodness you're back,' Maria said urgently, as Pippa burst through their bedroom door looking flustered. 'You've been in that bathroom for a month!'

'When was the last time you tried bathing this little toad by yourself!' Pippa said, as Twinkle bounded in behind her, sopping wet, but clean. 'She's a total fruit loop if you put her in water. If you think I look harassed, you should see the bathroom!'

'I'll go . . .' Sally said, fearing the wrath of Miss Coates if she found it in a mess.

'Just kidding,' Pippa giggled. 'Well, not about Twinkle making a mess . . . but don't worry, I cleared it up. Although I don't think there's a dry towel left anywhere at Garland!'

'Never mind all that!' Maria said, tapping her bed. 'Sit, sit, sit and talk, talk, talk! What happened out there tonight, Pips?'

Molly, Maria, Danya, Honey and Sally all sat poised to find out about the big, foggy, taking-down of Lucinda Marciano.

'Yes!' Sally said. 'I couldn't see a thing on the island through that fog, no matter how hard I looked through those super-duper binoculars of Maria's.'

'Well...' Pippa said, pausing to down the mug of steaming hot chocolate passed to her by Danya.

'Sorry! So, we saw Lucifette come out of the boathouse on her skates, but as we tried to follow her from a distance, we realised that we couldn't because the fog was actually getting worse by the second. We had to get closer and closer, just to stop losing sight of her completely . . .'

'Oh, my goodness, you must have been so worried she'd spot you following her,' Honey said, shovelling in a pink marshmallow.

'Exactly. And then we lost her . . .' Pippa started again.

'Lost her? What? Like lost her, lost her? Then how did you . . ?' Maria asked.

'Mimi, I love you, but would you please put a sock in it, and let Pippa tell her story!' Molly said.

'Sorry,' Maria muttered.

Pippa smiled.

'Yes, we lost her. Completely! And she wasn't the only thing that disappeared. Mr Hart suddenly noticed that with the fog getting higher and higher on the island, we could barely see the top of the bridge, let alone the snow cannon.

'We knew then that Sally's spotlight wouldn't be able to see anything, nor could I risk running back to you guys to say what had happened or I might have got lost in the fog myself. We had to stick together,' she paused again, feeling like Madame Ruby during her first assembly of the term speech.

'Gosh, it all sounds so terrifying, the fact that you couldn't see to put one foot in front of the other. One wrong move and you might have fallen in the lake or worse!' Honey said, grateful for the fact that her broken leg meant she hadn't been in any danger that night.

'It was . . . that is until we realised we had the most powerful piece of fog-beating equipment with us you could think of . . .'

'What?' the girls cried.

Woof! Twinkle barked proudly.

'Of course!' Maria and Danya said in unison, cottoning on straight away.

'Like Mr Hart said, who needs eyes when you have the best nose and ears in England! One word from him to find Lucifette and Twinkle was off . . . hot on her trail. Thank goodness he had her on a leash or she would have disappeared as well!' Pippa said.

'Oh, Twinkle, you are the best dog in the world,' Molly cooed, fondling her ears.

'She led us straight to the snow cannon, just in time to see Lucifette pour the last of the red dye in and start to leave. Except that she wasn't looking where she was going so fast on her skates and she crashed straight into me!'

The girls gasped.

'We both went flying!' Pippa said. 'And as we lay in a tangled mess on the grass, I heard the intro to the closing song start and the loudest WHOOOOSH you've ever heard as the snow cannon erupted, shooting a blast of red snow, right above our heads. We were covered from head to toe, straight away. And that's when Mr Hart ran at the cannon with all his might and rugby-tackled it to the ground, knocking it backwards so that the spray pointed away from the Glacier Palace . . .'

'Wow!' Honey said, picturing the scene perfectly from Pippa's vivid description.

'So that's how the snow never hit us!' Maria said. 'Clever, Mr Hart. And just in the nick of time too. That snow was a second away from covering L'Etoile and its guests in a scarlet blizzard.'

'But if Mr Hart was tied up with the snow cannon, that left you to wrestle with Lucifette. How did you manage to stop her from getting away?' Danya asked.

Woof! Woof! Twinkle barked, her tail wagging as though she understood every word.

'I swear this dog is human!' Sally squealed.

'I don't know about that, but she can be very fierce and persuasive when she wants to be. She had Lucinda pinned to the ground by her bonnet ribbons from the moment she hit the floor. Mind you, I'm not sure how much longer we could have stayed there without Mr Hart's help. If that snow cannon hadn't stopped when it did, I think Twinkle and I might have had a fight on our hands,' Pippa said.

'Cue Molly's brilliance!' Pippa said excitedly. 'Although, Moll, I have no idea how you knew where to find the power sockets!'

'Are you kidding?' Molly said. 'We were almost sitting on them! Thanks to Honey's leg!'

Honey smiled.

'The only thing I didn't know for sure was which cable to pull. Have you seen how many cables run in and out of that thing? I just followed the one which looked like it ran outside the building and went for it. It was pure luck!' Molly said.

'Well, I say you make your own luck, Miss Fitzfoster, and a little bit of genius and common sense goes a long way,' Danya said, dipping her hand into a jar of jelly beans.

'At the risk of putting a dampener on everything, I think our luck might just have run out where Madame Ruby is concerned. If my plan had worked, none of us would have come out having *red snow* on our hands. There's no way Mr Hart will be able to keep our names out of it now. It just got too complicated,' Maria moaned.

'Dad will be so disappointed. We promised him a clean, non-eventful term and we've managed to land ourselves in hot water yet again,' Molly said.

'Don't you mean iced water?' said Danya.

'Look, I wouldn't write us off just yet,' Pippa said, smiling.

'Really?' the girls asked at once.

'Really! Let's just say Mr Hart and I had just enough time to agree a story on the way back to the Glacier Palace, and thank goodness we did as we ran straight into Mrs Fuller. Believe me. By the time he's finished his report, I'll be written off as just having been in the wrong place at the wrong time and you girls won't even get a mention!'

'Oh, girls. Who would have believed it? A mystery solved, a disaster aborted and most importantly, two new members of the gang to celebrate,' Maria said happily.

'And I've got my sister back,' Molly whispered in Maria's ear before giving her the biggest hug.

'A toast then . . .' Honey said, reaching for her hot chocolate. 'To finding new friends, losing old enemies and having new adventures! Cheers!'

'Cheers!'

20

Home Time Again

'Right, so the snow cannon issue is a no-brainer. I'll just say there was a power surge or something. But what about the ghost, Helen?' Madame Ruby said, as she perched on the corner of her desk. 'I can't very well stand there and suggest the apparent paranormal activity at L'Etoile this term was due to a *technical fault*.'

Mrs Fuller thought for a moment. 'Look, Ruby. After hearing what Dad's had to say, I don't think we should be too specific or mention any names, but I do think that we should tell our side of the story, if only to reassure the parents that there is no ghost at the school. It would be far more damaging to leave any doubt in their minds than to say it was a student prank and that the student has since been dealt with.'

She turned to her father. 'At least, we can say, with all honesty, that apart from the girl in question, no other students were involved . . . except Pippa Burrows who happened to be in the wrong place at the wrong time tonight. I'm just thankful you were passing at the right time, Dad, and could step in to help. I always knew you had it in you to be the hero of the hour. You did a super job and quite literally saved the school from disaster.'

Mr Hart smiled.

'Yes, thank you, David,' Madame Ruby said. 'How's your shoulder? You should get Nurse Payne to check that over.'

Mr Hart winced. Not so much from shoulder pain but at the thought of going to see Nurse Payne. *No thank you very much.*

'If that's all then, I'll get off home. But I need to track Twinkle down first. I seem to have lost her between here and the rink,' he said, suddenly feeling exhausted.

'I think you'll find her snuggled up at Garland with the girls,' Mrs Fuller said. 'I didn't have the heart to prise them apart earlier so I cleared a *sleepover* with Miss Coates. Why don't you collect her in the morning? No ghosts to be scared of now, eh?'

'Night then, Helen,' he said and gave his daughter a kiss on the cheek. 'See you all tomorrow.

And he left Madame Ruby and his daughter to the eagerly waiting ears in the Ivy Room, relieved not to be in their shoes. He'd answered quite enough questions for one night and hoped that would be the end of it.

The last few days of term went by in a flurry. After the stresses and strains of the term, everyone was desperate to get home to their families.

'Can you believe we've got to this point and still not been connected with the whole *Lucifette the Ghost* case?' Danya said, as the girls all waited together on the drive.

'I'm so pleased for Mr Hart! Just look at him, he's still being congratulated wherever he goes,' Molly said, seeing Mr Hart practically blushing as parent after parent shook his hand.

'There's Eddie!' Maria cried, watching the old Fitzfoster Bentley bounce gently down the drive in their direction.

'Where will you be for the holidays, Honey?' Molly

asked, thinking how much she was going to miss her new friend.

'We usually go to Barbados, but I don't think we're going this year so it'll just be in London,' Honey answered.

'Barbados? No way! That's where we usually go. We're not this year as Mum and Dad offered the house to Mr and Mrs Fuller for their honeymoon as a wedding gift.

'How have we never bumped into you?' Danya asked, incredulous.

'I'd say it's because you twins have a lovely way of being in your own little worlds!' Pippa said. 'Or should I say planets!'

'Well, I love Planet Fitzfoster, and Planet Sawyer, and can think of nowhere I'd rather be,' Molly said. 'Maybe we could come and stay or something?'

'Yes!' Maria said quickly. I've got to be in London anyway as I'm doing my work experience at the Gazette with Luscious T!'

'OCYA!' Molly cried.

OCYA = Of Course You Are, Story-seeker

'How could I have forgotten? You must be beside yourself with excitement!'

'I will be when I get there. I'm terrified at the moment,' Maria said.

'You'll be terrific!' Danya said.

'Ditto!' Pippa agreed, spotting her Uncle Harry's car zooming down the drive. 'And just think – maybe you'll sniff out an adventure at the Gazette and find an excuse to get us all together!'

'That's my top priority!' Maria beamed, jumping back as Eddie pulled up alongside them.

'Good afternoon Miss Maria, Miss Molly and Miss Sally,' he said, always happy to be driving such precious cargo.

'Hi, Eddie!' Molly said, giving him a squeeze.

'Do I get one of those?' came a deep voice as the rear passenger window opened.

'Dad!' Maria cried. 'Mum! But what are you doing here? I thought we were seeing you at Wilton House?'

'We couldn't resist!' Brian Fitzfoster said, cuddling each of his girls in turn.

'We haven't seen you all term. Daddy and I just couldn't wait another hour!' Linda Fitzfoster said, smothering them in kisses. 'Oh, Molly. Just look at your arm. I can't believe you broke it and I wasn't there. Are you OK, darling?'

'I'm fine, Mum really. Could have been worse,' Molly said, glancing at Honey and her poor leg.

'And who are these two new faces?' Brian Fitzfoster asked, looking over at Danya and Honey.

'Dad! These girls are our new besties. The latest members of our elite gang!'

'I see,' Brian Fitzfoster smiled. 'And do these new *besties* have names?'

'I'm Danya,' Danya stepped forward. 'And this is my sister, Honey. We're twi…'

'Double trouble?' Mr Fitzfoster grinned. 'Yes, I'm well acquainted with double trouble. An expert on the subject you might say.'

'Oh, Dad! But we've been soooo good this term! Not an adventure between us!' Maria said, trying to look as innocent as she could.

'Hmmm,' Mr Fitzfoster thought for a moment. 'I don't really know what to do with that information. I'm not quite sure what to believe,' he said, looking at Molly's arm.

'Oh, Brian, leave the girls alone. Well, for now, at least. I have something much more fun to discuss,' Linda Fitzfoster said, handing envelopes to Pippa,

Sally, Molly and Maria. 'Mind you, I see I should have bought two extra invitations for Danya and Honey. I'll pop them in the post for you girls if you text your home address.'

The girls peeled open the flaps to reveal a golden lining and a small invitation card, which read:

> *FITZFOSTER UNDERGROUND PARTY*
> *VENUE: WILTON HOUSE – THE SECRET CAVE*
> *DATE: 24TH DECEMBER*
> *TIME: 6PM UNTIL LATE*
> *DRESS: JAMES BOND GLAMOUR*

'Oh, Mr and Mrs Fitzfoster. That sounds divine! Thank you so much,' Pippa said, breathless with excitement.

'It's of course for your mother and Uncle Harry too, Pippa,' Mrs Fitzfoster replied.

'Oh, my goodness, Dad. Are they finished? The renovations of the smugglers' cave? Is it ready?' Maria said.

'You just wait. You're in for the ride of your lives, girls!' Mr Fitzfoster said.

'Then what *are* we waiting for!' Maria said, diving into the back of the Bentley, followed by Molly and Sally. 'Call you tomorrow girls and we'll make a plan!' She waved to Danya, Honey and Pippa, who were getting into their cars.

'And what *plan* might that be, Maria Fitzfoster?' her dad asked suspiciously.

'Oh, I don't know, Dad, but we'll think of something!' Maria said with a wink and then under her breath . . . '*We always do!*'

A Guide to Molly Fitzfoster's Favourite Sayings

CO = Chill Out

WAYL = What Are You Like?

TDF = To Die For

AYKM = Are You Kidding Me?

WATC = What Are The Chances?

OCYA = Of Course You Are

the orion star